"So Cool on the Outside, So Warm Underneath . . ."

Adam threaded his fingers through the mass of her ash-blond hair.

This time there was no hesitation as their lips met in a searing kiss, a kiss that left its brand on them both. Long, strong fingers gently but firmly held her face up to his, covering the pulse at the base of her throat, tracing the vee of her blouse where it plunged downward toward the swell of her breasts.

Oh, dear God, Taylor thought desperately, this was crazy! She didn't want to want him. Her life was nicely planned and under control. There was simply no place in it for the disruptive influence of this man—or any man for that matter. But even as the thought crawled through her mind, she felt the velvety insistence of his tongue robbing her of both breath and conviction in the same instant. . . .

SUZANNE SIMMS

was born in Storm Lake, Iowa, and currently resides in Indiana with her husband and nine-year-old son. She has a degree in English literature, loves opera, and studied classical piano for ten years. Ms. Simms loves reading and writing romances and believes being a successful romance writer is primarily a matter of attitude.

Dear Reader:

SILHOUETTE DESIRE is an exciting new line of contemporary romances from Silhouette Books. During the past year, many Silhouette readers have written in telling us what other types of stories they'd like to read from Silhouette, and we've kept these comments and suggestions in mind in developing SILHOUETTE DESIRE.

DESIREs feature all of the elements you like to see in a romance, plus a more sensual, provocative story. So if you want to experience all the excitement, passion and joy of falling in love, then SILHOUETTE DESIRE is for you.

I hope you enjoy this book and all the wonderful stories to come from SILHOUETTE DESIRE. I'd appreciate any thoughts you'd like to share with us on new SILHOUETTE DESIRE, and I invite you to write to us at the address below:

Karen Solem
Editor-in-Chief
Silhouette Books
P.O. Box 769
New York, N.Y. 10019

SUZANNE SIMMS
So Sweet A Madness

Silhouette Desire

Published by Silhouette Books New York

America's Publisher of Contemporary Romance

Other Silhouette Books by Suzanne Simms

Moment in Time
Of Passion Born
A Wild, Sweet Magic
All the Night Long

SILHOUETTE BOOKS, a Division of Simon & Schuster, Inc.
1230 Avenue of the Americas, New York, N.Y. 10020

Copyright © 1983 by Suzanne Guntrum

Distributed by Pocket Books

ISBN: 0-671-46356-X

First Silhouette Books printing August, 1983

10 9 8 7 6 5 4 3 2 1

America's Publisher of Contemporary Romance

Printed in the U.S.A.

Dedicated to those very special friends—
Jayne, Barbara, and Elaine

So Sweet
A Madness

1

~~~~~~~~~~~~~~~~~~~~~~

Whistling a nameless tune under his breath, Detective Lieutenant Adam McCord opened the door of Knoxville's Civic Auditorium and stepped inside. Quickly downing the last of his coffee, he tossed the empty styrofoam cup in a trash container by the entrance. Although he was officially off duty for the rest of the night he'd decided to take a look at the place on his way home.

He stood there a moment at the back of the large hall, one hand running through his thick, brown hair in an absent-minded gesture, the other casually resting on his hip. The jacket of his dark suit strained against his broad shoulders, his typically male stance clearly revealing the muscular physique beneath the material.

Halfway down the aisle he stopped dead in his tracks. In quick succession his gaze swept the auditori-

um, the well-lighted stage with its row upon row of
empty chairs, and finally the solitary figure of a woman
seated center stage.

From this distance the woman appeared to be fairly
tall and on the slender side, her features concealed by
a drape of long, blond hair as she leaned over the
music stand in front of her. He hadn't expected to find
anyone but the night watchman here at this hour. He
certainly never expected to find a woman all alone. As
he opened his mouth to call out to her, she positioned
her hands and gracefully drew the bow across the
cello cradled between her legs.

Adam McCord would be the first to admit that his
knowledge of classical music was limited. In fact, he
thought most of it was dull, even tedious; his personal
taste inclined more to the country-western ballad or
the popular rock style of Neil Diamond. But as the
plaintive, almost human voice of the cello carried from
one end of the auditorium to the other he found
himself captivated by the sound.

It didn't take an expert to recognize that the cellist
was good, very good, whoever she was. The man
stood there, watching and listening, caught up in the
strangely intimate spell cast by the deserted concert
hall, the vision of a woman with shimmering, ash-
blond hair, and the truly incredible music coming from
the solitary string instrument. It was a moment he
knew would be indelibly stamped on his memory.

When the final note faded away the woman slowly
raised her head and peered into the shadows. She
seemed to sense that she was no longer alone. From
his vantage point Adam McCord could see she was
younger than he had originally thought, certainly
something less than his own thirty-two years. Her

features were boldly drawn, striking in their appearance, possessing perhaps more character than actual beauty.

"That was beautiful," he commented, walking down the aisle toward her, his own deep baritone amplified by the near-perfect acoustics of the place.

He stopped directly in front of the stage and looked up at her. Her face was clearly visible now. He could see that her eyes were an extraordinary shade of gray, smoke-colored with blue-green rims around the irises. There was an alabaster cast to her complexion that gave her skin a translucent quality. Amidst the ivory smoothness of her face the cheekbones were high and lightly tinged with color, the nose straight and slightly dramatic, the mouth sensuously full above the curve of her chin.

Her back never once touched the chair behind it, adding a fullness to her breasts and a certain regality to her posture. He could almost imagine the hundreds of times she had been told as a child to "sit up straight." After all, a *lady* simply did not slouch.

On closer inspection, he saw she was fully as slender as he had first thought, but not as tall. She could be no more than five feet four inches at most. It was his business to know these things and Lieutenant Adam McCord was very good at his business.

But it was her hands that fascinated him. The nails were buffed and necessarily clipped close, the fingers long and agile, graceful even in their slightest movement. They were, in truth, the hands of an artist.

She looked at him for a minute or two without speaking, as though taking her own measure of the man who had seemingly emerged out of nowhere. Apparently, he passed whatever test she was silently subjecting him to for a tentative smile appeared on her face.

"You like Debussy then," she said in a low, rich alto, nodding her head as she spoke.

"Debussy?" His brows drew together.

"Claude Debussy, the composer of the sonata I was practicing," she went on to explain, a genuinely puzzled expression on her face, as if it hadn't occurred to her that he could possibly be unfamiliar with the piece of music she'd been playing.

"Oh—*that* Debussy!" he mocked lightly.

The woman's attitude became perceptibly more cautious. "Are you looking for someone in particular?" she asked, fingering the sheets of music in front of her in an agitated fashion.

"No—I'm not looking for anyone in particular. At least not tonight." Adam could tell that his unintentionally vague reply did little to reassure her that he meant no harm. "I'm Lieutenant McCord of the Knoxville Police Department, Investigations Division." He took his I.D. from the breast pocket of his suit and held it out for her inspection.

"You're a policeman?" Her gray eyes widened in surprise.

"Yes, I am," he drawled, trying not to show his amusement. It wasn't the first time his profession had elicited such a reaction. "I wanted to take a preliminary look at the auditorium before the concert next week. We're expecting the British ambassador to attend."

"Then you're officially involved in providing police protection for the concert," she said, her brows drawn in a thoughtful frown.

His nod was succinctly professional. "I'll be working

in conjunction with federal authorities, of course. I assume you're a member of the Knoxville Symphony Orchestra, Miss—"

"Jameson. Taylor Jameson. And, yes, I'm a violoncellist with the Symphony, *Lieutenant.*" He thought he heard her sniff indignantly.

"You're very good, too, from what I just heard," he remarked, returning the I.D. to his breast pocket.

She turned a beautifully innocent gaze on him. "Why, thank you, Lieutenant." She glanced at her wristwatch. "But isn't it a little late for you to be out safeguarding our fair city?"

His broad shoulders rose in an expressive shrug. "You know what they say, Miss Jameson—a policeman's work is never done."

"I'm afraid I wouldn't know about that, Lieutenant," she said loftily. "I've never met a policeman before."

"The name is Adam McCord," he told her, his voice deep and his words deliberately spaced, "and *I* have never met a cello player before."

"Somehow that doesn't surprise me," she mumbled.

His gaze never faltered. "I apologize if I interrupted your practice."

Taylor made an airy little gesture with her hand, dismissing both the man and his apology in the process. "Oh, you didn't interrupt anything. It's time I was leaving anyway."

That much, at least, was true. It *was* time she was leaving. Good Lord, her watch said nearly eleven o'clock! The other members of the string quartet had gone home over an hour ago. She'd meant to stay only long enough to run through the Debussy sonata and Piston's Trio. Somehow she had lost track of the time. And she still had that stack of papers in her briefcase to correct!

Quickly getting to her feet, she began to pack the bow and cello away in their carrying case. As she did, Taylor noticed that her hands were trembling. She hated to admit it, but the man's unexpected appearance had shaken her. She supposed she should be thankful he'd turned out to be a policeman, even if he was a rather ignorant one. The absolute nerve of the man calling *her* a *cello player!*

"May I help you carry that to your car, Miss Jameson?" With a well-executed leap he was up on the stage and attempting to relieve her of the cumbersome carrying case.

"Thank you, but *no.*" She politely but firmly put him in his place, refusing to relinquish her hold on it. "I've managed well enough without your help for fifteen years, Lieutenant McCord. Besides," she said sweetly, "I wouldn't dream of troubling you with a little thing like a cello when you must have official duties that require your attention elsewhere."

"It's no trouble," he persisted. "After all, I am a public servant here to aid and defend the citizens of Knoxville." When that line of reasoning seemed destined to fail, he tried a different tactic. "Consider it a return on your investment then." Taylor raised her brows in a questioning arch. "Your tax dollars pay my salary, Miss Jameson." Then he smiled, a smile that transformed what she had thought of as rather ordinary features into something quite extraordinary.

Squelching a strong desire to tell him exactly what he could do with his offer of help, she grudgingly accepted, "Well, when you put it that way . . ." Taylor watched as the carrying case was neatly taken from her grasp. "I can see you're the type who insists on helping little old ladies cross the street whether they want to or not," she said, disgruntled.

"I've been known to on occasion." He smiled and again she felt the impact. "But I prefer to come to the rescue of young women with shapely legs, long, blond hair and arresting gray eyes," he finished, flicking his gaze from her thighs to her face.

"And I've always liked a man in uniform," she purred softly, determined to give tit for tat.

"But I don't wear a uniform." The detective frowned, rubbing his jaw.

"Yes—I know," she said dryly, turning to gather up her music. She tucked it under her arm and looked up at him. "I'm ready if you are, Lieutenant."

"After you, Miss Jameson," he insisted with what sounded suspiciously like a chuckle. She was beginning to wonder if anything could burst Lieutenant Adam McCord's bubble!

As she led the way down the steps at the far end of the stage, Taylor found herself annoyingly aware of the man. Damn him, he was managing the heavy violoncello as if it were a toy! And to think of all the times she'd struggled with its unwieldy size simply to get it in and out of her car. No easy task for a woman barely five feet four inches tall and one hundred and ten pounds.

Of course, if she were honest with herself—and honesty was one thing Taylor insisted on—she had to admit that it was hardly his fault he was bigger and stronger than she. It was just so darned frustrating at times. Not that she would change a moment of the past fifteen years; she wouldn't. The cello had been a major part of her life for too long now. In fact, she scarcely thought of it as separate from herself.

Perhaps it was the same for this man and the gun he no doubt carried with him at all times. She hadn't thought of it in quite that way before, but she supposed it was true. A policeman might well consider his gun a natural extension of himself. The thought sent a chill down her spine. The violoncello was an instrument of beauty, the gun, one of destruction. And therein lay the real difference between her world and that of the man walking beside her.

"Do you carry a gun?" The words came from Taylor almost unconsciously.

He seemed surprised by the question. "I haven't heard it called a gun in a long time, but, yes, I do carry one."

Taylor had thought she would be repelled; instead she found herself fascinated with the idea that this man could be dangerous. This was a glimpse into a world she'd never even imagined, much less seen.

"Do you like being a policeman?" she asked as they walked up the center aisle of the auditorium toward the door.

Lieutenant McCord merely smiled and shrugged. "I don't think *like* is quite the right word. I believe in what I'm doing. At least most of the time. You see, being a cop is kind of a tradition in my family."

"A tradition?" She interrupted him quietly.

"Yes. My father was a policeman and his father before him. I've more or less carried on the tradition, although I was the first member of my family to graduate from college."

Taylor was genuinely interested now. "And where was that?"

"Back in Pittsburgh," he answered, pushing the door open and allowing her to precede him into the warm September night.

"I played Pittsburgh once," she said. "I'll always remember getting on the airplane for that trip. They actually strapped my cello into the seat beside mine. The minute the cabin personnel saw me and my cello, I could almost feel their hostility. I felt guilty for having it on board, even though I'd had to pay half fare for it." She shook her head as if to dislodge the memory. "So, you're from Pittsburgh."

"Yep, I was not only born and raised there, but spent the first thirty years of my life in the city." His voice trailed off into a nostalgic silence.

Taylor turned to look at him. "How did you end up in Knoxville then?"

He gave her a guarded answer. "I came through on a trip to the Great Smoky Mountains one time. I'd been wanting a change of scenery anyway and discovered I really liked Knoxville. I've been here almost two years now." She had the strangest feeling the story had been whitewashed for her benefit, but she could hardly call the bluff of a total stranger. "You don't sound like a native yourself," Adam speculated.

"I'm originally from St. Louis, but I've worked and lived in Knoxville for the past five years." She stopped under a streetlight long enough to get her keys from her handbag. "My car is over there." She indicated the only other vehicle in the parking lot besides his.

"I would never have guessed," he teased, walking straight for the late-model station wagon. "Kind of an odd choice for a single woman, isn't it?"

"Not when she has to haul a rather good-sized cello with her wherever she goes," Taylor replied in a dry voice, unlocking the tailgate.

"Well, they say necessity is the mother of invention," he drawled, stowing the carrying case in the back. "There was a woman in our old neighborhood in Pittsburgh who bought a station wagon just so she could haul her dogs around in it."

"Haul her dogs around?" she heard herself echo.

"She claimed they loved riding in a car. Since she had almost a dozen animals of every size and description, she figured a station wagon was the only answer. It was a damned funny sight, I'll tell you, to see Mrs. McCollough drive down the street with a carload of dogs hanging their noses out of every available window." His warm laughter seemed to scatter the night shadows hovering over the dark parking lot.

Taylor was surprised to hear her own laughter join his. "I'll admit I've gotten a few funny looks myself," she bantered, closing the rear door of the car.

The man seemed to be digging around in the pocket of his suit coat for something. She couldn't make it out in the dim light. "Would you like a piece of bubble gum?" he finally asked, extending his hand palm up.

"Bubble gum?" She burst out laughing, then broke off when she realized he was perfectly serious.

"I've been trying to quit smoking," he confessed with a sheepish expression on his face. "I figure it's almost impossible to smoke and chew bubble gum at the same time."

"Thank you, but I don't care for any," Taylor politely refused.

"Ah, c'mon, I bet it's been years since you had a piece of bubble gum." Adam unwrapped a piece and tossed it into his mouth. "So, who's going to see you being a little less than dignified out here at this time of night?" he cajoled, inadvertently hitting the nail squarely on the head.

For in many ways Taylor Jameson's life was indeed a study in dignity. Dignity and discipline. They were the key words in her personal as well as her professional life. Always one to say and do the correct thing, she was a woman who rarely let herself go. When she did, it was only in her music.

Yet the almost boyish dare issued by Adam McCord struck a responsive chord deeply buried beneath the layers of sophistication.

"All right, Lieutenant," she said, finally relenting and putting her hand out. She unwrapped the piece of gum and carefully placed half of it into her mouth.

"That wasn't so bad, was it?" His voice was gritty, entirely masculine. "Now if I could only get you to drop the 'Lieutenant' business and call me Adam. . . ."

Taylor had known all along that her persistent use of his title irritated the man. Why she would want to arouse such an emotion in a perfect stranger was a mystery to her. But she had the oddest sensation they were somehow embroiled in an age-old battle without either their prior consent or approval.

Perhaps it had something to do with the element of danger Adam McCord represented. Most men left her cold; they were unable to arouse either like or dislike in her, let alone curiosity. But she was curious about this man. God alone knew why. And just how long could she go on referring to him as "Lieutenant" when they stood there chomping on bubble gum like a couple of school kids?

"All right then, *Adam,*" she said, lifting her chin in unspoken challenge.

He seemed to immediately sense her capitulation and pushed a step further. "There's a place not far from here that still serves a good cup of coffee at this hour. Why don't you join me?"

Taylor almost swallowed her gum. "I-I'm afraid that's impossible."

His brow arched in query. "Impossible?"

"I have an early class in the morning and a stack of papers to correct yet tonight," she hastened to explain.

He was very quiet for a moment. "You're a teacher?"

She could feel his eyes on her. "Yes, I teach in the music department at the University."

There was an odd little silence. "Good God, you're a college professor." He gave a short, dry laugh.

"Yes, I am, among other things," Taylor retorted, mildly annoyed.

He ran a hand through his thick, dark hair. "I guess I figured you worked full-time for the Symphony."

"The Knoxville Symphony has a core of sixteen full-time musicians, but I enjoy teaching as well," she said with a touch of reproach.

"In that case, Professor," Adam neatly lifted the car keys from her hand and unlocked the station wagon, "it's late. Time you were going home." In a final, gallant gesture he opened the door of the car.

A look of vexation passed over Taylor's face. "I won't call you 'Lieutenant,' if you promise not to call me 'Professor,'" she retorted, settling herself behind the wheel. She turned on the ignition and hit the button to lower the power window on her side. "I-I want to thank you for the help with my cello." It was a rather belated "thank you," she realized.

Adam put his hand on the window with apparent casualness. "It was my pleasure," he said, looking intently into her eyes.

"I'm playing in a string quartet recital at the University tomorrow evening. If you'd like to come, perhaps we could have that cup of coffee afterwards," she said impulsively.

She noticed a subtle change in his eyes. He seemed as surprised by the invitation as she was herself. "All right, I would like that."

"It's at eight o'clock in the recital hall in the main complex," she went on hurriedly, not knowing what had possessed her to extend the invitation in the first place. She was not a woman who normally acted on impulse.

"Then I'll see you after the recital tomorrow night," he said, holding her eyes a moment longer.

"Good night, Adam McCord," she said primly, again pushing the button for the power window.

She saw rather than heard his parting words as it closed. "Good night, Taylor Jameson."

He was still standing there when she turned on the headlights and pulled out of the parking lot.

It was an unusually warm, hazy night for mid-September. Suddenly, all Taylor wanted was to get home to her cool, air-conditioned apartment and kick off her shoes. It had been another grueling, sixteen-hour day and she was bone tired.

She had gone several blocks when some sixth sense

warned her she was being followed. At first she refused to believe it was anything but coincidence or an overactive imagination. That was what she told herself until she stopped for a red light and glanced in the rear-view mirror. The nondescript gray sedan was still right behind her. Then the faint glow from a cigarette lighter illuminated the face of the driver and she saw that it was none other than Adam McCord.

Apparently, chewing bubble gum as a deterrent to smoking wasn't all it was cracked up to be, she thought to herself with a wry smile. Then she was puzzled. There was no earthly reason for him to be following her—unless, of course, he lived in this direction himself. She had gone several more blocks before she was convinced that he had every intention of following her right to her doorstep.

That was ridiculous! If he was so anxious to find out where she lived, then he could damn well look up her address in the telephone book like everyone else. She was clearly listed as T. Jameson, 24 Kenton Place. It didn't take a Philadelphia lawyer to figure that one out!

It had been a mistake to invite him to the recital. She could see that already. She was hardly in the habit of taking up with strangers, and for good reason. After all, what did she know about him other than the fact that he was thirty-two years old and came from Pittsburgh.

Good Lord, she was beginning to sound paranoid. The man was a police officer. What could he do to her if she refused to "cooperate"? Arrest her? And she had rather liked his smile. It gave Adam McCord's features a devastating quality that was not immediately apparent. He seemed like a perfectly harmless sort.

Now she *was* getting fanciful. Harmless? Not with those broad shoulders and bedroom eyes. The truth, she supposed, was somewhere in between the two extremes.

At the next red light Taylor surreptitiously glanced in the rear-view mirror again. He was still there, his tanned face looking rather serious from what she could see, the thatch of dark hair barely visible in the faint light shining through his car window.

It was a little late to pull her car over and announce she was withdrawing her invitation, so she'd just have to make the best of it. One quick cup of coffee after the recital and she'd be on her way, and Lieutenant Adam McCord could be on his!

Turning onto Walnut Street, Taylor accelerated up the steep hill that eventually leveled off at Kenton Place. Several blocks to the right was the Blakley House, a renowned hotel. Nearby were several excellent restaurants including the Union Cafe and Piccolo's.

Kenton Place itself was a row of recently renovated red-brick townhouses. Taylor loved the two-story dwelling she had purchased only the year before. Driving up to the wrought-iron gates, she pressed the button to open them just as Adam McCord pulled alongside in his car.

She put her window down and came straight to the point. "Why are you following me?"

His face broke into a smile. "I just wanted to make sure you got home all right. Haven't you ever heard of a police escort?" With that, he touched a hand to his forehead in a brief salute and backed out of the driveway.

Taylor was left sitting there literally speechless. In

the game of one-upmanship, she had to concede *that* point went to Adam McCord. Mumbling under her breath, she drove through the gates of Kenton Place and parked in front of number 24.

Ten minutes later she was locking the door behind her as she set her briefcase on the hall table and kicked off her shoes. The apartment was cool and dark except for one lamp left burning in the living room. Though the townhouse was a two-story building, it consisted of only four rooms, a large living area and kitchen downstairs and two bedrooms and a bath above.

The original hardwood floors had been preserved throughout. The living room was light and airy in feeling; pale turquoise paper with a subtle basket-weave design covered the walls. The same basket-weave print was echoed in the off-white, scalloped-edged wing chairs on either side of the mantel. A white raw-silk sofa sat in front of two large windows, also draped in off-white. The accent colors of pale turquoise and melon were repeated in an armless chair and an assortment of throw pillows. A brightly striped rag rug broke the gleaming expanse of dark, hardwood floor.

The total effect was chic and feminine, without the usual cluttered look professional decorators seemed so fond of. At the far end of the room sat a baby grand piano, a graduation gift from Taylor's parents when she received her Master of Music degree some five years before. Like many young, gifted musicians, she had played the piano as her first instrument; her special love and ability for the cello were discovered when she was in her early teens.

Following her usual nightly routine, Taylor put a

kettle of water on to heat while she sorted through the day's mail. When it proved to contain little of interest she made herself a cup of tea and settled down on the sofa with her briefcase. Halfway through the first essay on Haydn's Concerto in D Major for Cello and Orchestra, she discovered that her mind was wandering. Her thoughts were of a broad-shouldered, brown-eyed man with a rather disconcerting smile.

Taylor brought herself up short. "Oh, no, you don't, Adam McCord!" she vowed out loud.

She was not about to allow him into her life in any way, shape or form. At the age of twenty-seven she was too smart to ask for *that* kind of trouble. Her goals for the future were clearly set and she knew exactly what it would take to achieve them. There was simply no room in her life for the disruptive influence of a man, least of all one who couldn't even begin to sympathize with her chosen career.

Oh, she'd been in love before. Truly, madly in love. Or so she had thought at the time. Although he had been a musician himself, he had found it impossible to accept Taylor's devotion to her music. The experience had taught her an invaluable lesson. No man was content to play second fiddle to a woman's aspirations.

Someone like Adam McCord could never understand what it took to be a classical musician. The years of study and practice, the mental and physical concentration, the numerous evenings required in a concert hall—they all added up to a uniquely demanding lifestyle quite unlike any other. The nearest thing Taylor could equate it to was the ballet. It took the same intense dedication to be a dancer as it did to be a musician.

She was confident that one day she would attain her goal. She would be the principal cellist with a major symphony orchestra. She had tried a year of touring on her own and found it a grueling, sobering experience. Too few people appreciated the cello as a solo instrument. Too many nights in a seemingly endless string of hotel rooms had taught her she wasn't cut out for the life of a concert artist.

But there were alternatives as long as she remained true to the course she had set for herself. From the beginning she had known the sacrifices required of her and she had willingly made them. To seek excellence in any form was a lonely business, but the rewards were great. To be musically talented was a rare gift, and Taylor Jameson wasn't about to throw it away for anyone or anything.

There were times, of course, when she missed what the majority of women her age took for granted. She had a few close friends from her days at the conservatory, but most of them were scattered across the country and even in Europe now. During those restless moments, which she somehow thought of as "spring fever" whatever the season, Taylor acknowledged a temptation to feel a pair of strong arms about her, a warm body beside hers. It was a temptation that she dismissed with her usual cynicism about such things. She might be a woman with a woman's needs and desires, but she was first and foremost a musician.

Well, musician or not, she was going to bed! She might as well, Taylor grumbled, snapping the gum back into her mouth after executing a particularly fine bubble. She wasn't getting anywhere with the Haydn essays for Music 422 anyway.

A creature of meticulous habits, she dispensed with

the now tasteless piece of bubble gum and cleared away her teacup and briefcase before calling it a night. Once upstairs, she made herself brush her teeth and cream the light-brown mascara from her lashes before she slipped into her nightgown.

It took only a few minutes of tossing and turning for Taylor Jameson to realize she was not going to fall asleep. Experience had taught her it was useless to fight it, so she turned the light on and reached for the remote control of the small television at the foot of her bed.

One click and several moments later, she realized she was watching a late-night rerun of an old police series. She flicked the button to another channel. This time it took her at least five minutes to figure out how a team of highly acrobatic thieves intended to steal the crown jewels from the Tower of London.

Good grief, all that was missing were the Keystone Cops! Was it always nonstop cops and robbers on television at this hour? Well, she for one had had about enough of the law for one night. Her expression was disdainful as she clicked off the set and turned over.

But as she lay there in that nether world between wakefulness and sleep, the face Taylor saw in the darkness was that of a smiling policeman named Adam McCord. . . .

2

~~~~~~~~~~~

Damn!" Adam McCord swore under his breath as he settled his six-foot-plus frame into an aisle seat at the back of the recital hall. The concert had started promptly at eight o'clock. Despite his best intentions it was almost nine now. He had somehow managed to miss the entire first hour.

But that wasn't what bothered him. What did was the distinct possibility that Taylor might think he wasn't coming at all. Basic human intuition told him one didn't stand up a woman like Taylor Jameson and then expect to be forgiven for it. She didn't strike him as the forgiving type. Hell, he'd be willing to bet his last dollar she was one of those people who was never late for anything!

Adam sat half-sprawled in his seat, seemingly unaware of the air of assured masculinity he exuded as naturally as most men just breathe. The slightly rumpled brown business suit he wore would have been unflattering on a less virile man, a man with anything less than his hard-muscled physique.

They were a dime a dozen, those dressed to perfection, smooth as glass, dapper men—but Adam McCord was definitely not one of them. He had neither the time nor the inclination—not to mention the money—to indulge in making himself a fashion plate. He did a tough job the best way he knew how. His aim was to look presentable, not like some damned silly male model.

The houselights blinked several times in quick succession, signaling that the intermission was over and the concert about to resume. As the lights dimmed one last time, the undercurrent of conversation in the hall gave way to polite silence. Then there was a respectable round of applause as Taylor Jameson walked out on the stage with her cello in hand.

The effect was surprisingly dramatic. She was dressed in a black, silky creation that fell in graceful folds to her ankles. As she walked, a bit of slender leg could be seen above her strappy black heels. Her hair was swept up into a glorious blond halo secured with a set of ebony combs, her only jewelry a single strand of milky-white pearls. To Adam she was a vision of elegance and serenity, a creature of another time and place.

Without a word she took the seat positioned several feet from the concert grand as a young man took his place at the keyboard. There was an electrifying moment of anticipation and then with a slight nod of her head, Taylor raised her bow and began to play.

Once again Adam McCord found himself caught up in the spell she wove, but this time he wasn't alone.

Every member of the audience seemed to be sitting forward in their seats, as if they somehow sensed that there was indeed something special about this woman and the music she made.

It took him a minute or two to realize she was performing the same melodic music he had heard her play the night before at the Civic Auditorium. He peered down at the program in his hand and made out the words "Sonata for Cello and Piano (No. 1) by Claude Debussy." It was in two parts, a short Prologue followed by a Serenade and Finale. One additional note stated it had been written in 1915 in homage to Debussy's wife, Emma.

Well, he might not know much about either the composer or the music, but he didn't need to in order to appreciate the fact that he was hearing a performance by a world-class musician. The audience was as still as any he had ever seen. Apparently, people with a far greater knowledge of classical music than he recognized that this was not an average, run-of-the-mill recital.

For some inexplicable reason, Adam McCord felt a surge of personal pride in the woman performing. The dreamy, sensuous music was weaving its spell over them all. They were eagerly, willingly its captives, as surely as they were hers.

The sonata wasn't a lengthy piece—it was under fifteen minutes by Adam's calculations. When the final note was sounded there was a momentary pause before the applause broke loose. Taylor looked up with an oddly dreamy smile on her face. She gave a self-conscious little nod in response and rose from her chair.

As the last smattering of applause died away,

another woman and two men joined her on stage, each carrying their music and respective instruments. A quick glance at the program confirmed that there were two violins and a viola in addition to the cello, completing the string quartet.

Adam would have liked to have said later that he heard every note of the Haydn quartet that was performed as the final selection of the evening, but, in truth, he did not. He found his attention riveted to the form, the hands, the face of Taylor Jameson alone. There was no doubt in his mind that she was unlike any woman he had ever known.

It was almost as if she were having some sort of love affair with her music. To think of all that warmth, all that passion and sensitivity lying just below the surface, hidden by the cool exterior she presented to the world. To think of the gentle but firm touch of those hands stroking him as they were now stroking the instrument within their grasp. The thought was definitely intoxicating. It left him feeling rather heady.

When the concert came to an end Adam unfurled his tall form from the seat and patiently stood there as the rest of the audience filed past him. Taylor's name was mentioned more than once, always with praise for her artistry and the sheer beauty of the cello as an instrument to watch as well as to listen to. With the hall nearly empty, he made his way toward the front. His long, powerful strides carried him down the aisle and around to the stage door.

Taylor didn't see him at first. She was busy putting her music away until Andrea Martin gave her a meaningful nudge with her elbow.

"Well, well, would you take a look at that," the statuesque brunette drawled with feminine curiosity.

"Take a look at what?" Taylor innocently asked, raising her head to glance in the direction Andrea herself was staring. A perfectly round circle formed on her mouth, but no sound was forthcoming. Adam was standing in the wings, waiting until she had gathered up her things. She hadn't been certain until that moment that he had even come.

"Definitely the macho type, wouldn't you say?" Andrea murmured, the violin in her hand all but forgotten. Without an ounce of compunction, she was looking Adam McCord over from head to toe.

Pretending an offhandedness she didn't feel, Taylor went back to the task of collecting her music. "I suppose you could say he's the macho type." Actually, seeing Adam through the eyes of another woman made her realize there was something about the man. . . .

Andrea Martin was many things herself, but slow wasn't one of them. "Do you know him?" she pressed Taylor, suddenly suspicious.

"Yes, as a matter of fact, I do," she replied with a proprietary tone in her voice.

That seemed to settle the question of the man's availability. Rumor had it Andrea Martin made a hobby of collecting men. In fact, at the age of thirty she was something of a connoisseur, but even a connoisseur had her limits. Andrea's was never to get involved with another woman's man—unless, of course, he was willing.

"Well, speaking from personal experience"— Andrea Martin's was no doubt plentiful—"I'd say you've got your hands full with that one, my dear Taylor. Shoulders like his should be against the law. Not to mention the rest of him."

Taylor Jameson pulled herself up to her full five feet four inches and looked the other woman straight in the eye. "My dear Andrea, he is the law."

The violinist's mouth opened and closed several times. "Do you mean to tell me he's a—a . . ."

". . . policeman." Taylor supplied the missing word.

"A policeman! Are you in some kind of trouble?"

"Of course I'm not in any trouble," Taylor laughingly reassured her.

A deliberately skeptical brow was raised. "Is he a friend of yours then?"

"Not exactly," she hedged, suddenly reluctant to admit she barely knew the man in question.

As if on cue, Adam McCord inclined his head in a slight nod and strolled toward them. He didn't stop until he was standing directly in front of Taylor. Something warned her he was fully aware of the subject of their conversation if not the actual content, but it was too late now to worry about that.

"You were superb as usual," Adam said a little dryly, gazing down at her with slight wariness.

Much to her surprise, Taylor was genuinely pleased to see him. "Thank you, Adam," she replied with more warmth than she had originally planned. "I hope you enjoyed the concert."

His tanned face dissolved into a smile. "I enjoyed you," he murmured, his deep voice softening slightly. His hand closed around hers with an easy masculine strength. "I recognized the Debussy sonata from last night," he added rather proudly.

Taylor bit her lip. "Did you?" She suddenly wondered if it was her imagination or if indeed the man was thinking of kissing her right then and there. "Oh—excuse me," she apologized, tearing her gaze from his. Under the circumstances, an introduction seemed unavoidable. "Andrea Martin—Lieutenant Adam McCord." She purposely failed to expound on either relationship.

"Lieutenant—" the brunette drawled in a sultry voice. It was amazing how much a woman like Andrea could convey in a single word.

"Miss Martin." Adam acknowledged Andrea's unspoken invitation with more than a touch of drollness.

Andrea's dark-eyed gaze moved over the man. "So you enjoyed our little recital, Lieutenant."

"Yes, I did, very much," he said smoothly. He seemed about to say more and then changed his mind. Exerting a subtle pressure on Taylor's hand, he urged her closer. "Are you ready to go?" As his eyes came back to hers she could almost feel their warmth penetrating her skin, compelling her body to react.

"Just give me a minute to finish putting my things away," she said a little breathlessly, several sheets of music fluttering from her grasp.

"I've never known you to be a butterfingers," the other woman pointed out, handing Taylor a sheet that had landed at her feet.

"Normally, I'm not," she muttered ungraciously. It was all Adam McCord's fault. He was the one who insisted on looking at her like *that*. "Thank you, Andrea," she added belatedly as Adam relieved her of the carrying case. "I'll see you tomorrow night at rehearsal."

"I'm sure you'll excuse us, Miss Martin," he said pleasantly enough, putting his hand on Taylor's shoulder with apparent casualness. She found herself secretly pleased that the statuesque brunette had made little if any impression on him. That alone made Adam

McCord unique among men. And Taylor liked him all the more for it.

Neither spoke again until they were outside in the parking lot. "Your car or mine?" Adam quipped with good humor.

"Yours *and* mine," Taylor replied, heading straight for the blue station wagon. "It'll be a lot easier if we both drive. That way we won't have to come back to the University later."

"I guess that makes sense," he muttered, not altogether pleased with the arrangement.

"Of course it does," she said as he loaded the cello in her car.

"How about stopping at a little coffee shop I know of on Market?" Adam suggested. "That way you won't have far to drive to get home."

"Sounds fine to me," Taylor said in a brisk tone. "You lead, I'll follow," she added hastily.

"That's the way I've always preferred it," Adam drawled, suppressing a grin. He couldn't, however, hide a brief smile as he turned and walked toward the gray sedan parked a short distance from her station wagon.

He was laughing at her. The man was actually laughing at *her!* Well, came the haughty thought, as far as she was concerned Detective Lieutenant Adam McCord had two chances of ever seeing her again— *fat* and *slim!* He'd just have to get his laughs someplace else. She had provided enough amusement for his benefit.

Back to square one, Taylor thought, turning on the ignition and following him out of the lot. A quick cup of coffee and that would be the end of their relationship. What in the world was she saying? They had no relationship. One cup of coffee and they could and *would* go their separate ways.

The traffic on Cumberland wasn't bad at this time of night. She found she could easily keep Adam's car in view. In tandem they pulled into a lot on the corner and parked side by side. He was waiting to open the door on the driver's side when she reached to unlock it.

"Thank you," she said in a petulant voice, her silk skirt swishing about her legs as she stepped out of the car.

"You're welcome," Adam replied, throwing her a puzzled glance.

It was no more than half a city block to the coffee shop. Taylor was aware of Adam's hand just behind her elbow every step of the way, although he was careful not to actually touch her. As they walked, she studied him out of the corner of her eye, noting the strength of his profile, the breadth of those shoulders everyone seemed to notice on first meeting, the cut of his jaw.

It wasn't a kind face, she remarked to herself, although she didn't know why that should matter to her. Just as those broad shoulders didn't matter. Although from his point of view, they no doubt came in handy when Adam was up against the unsavory types he encountered in his line of work. She couldn't begin to imagine doing a job such as his on a daily basis.

It wasn't that Taylor was naive. She knew well enough that the world could be an ugly, cruel place. She simply chose not to wallow in that side of life. The world could be beautiful as well, and she preferred beauty to ugliness. She supposed some people would say she led a sheltered life, but it always annoyed her when that observation was made on the basis of her occupation, or worse, her physical appearance.

Her looks—ethereal, blond, fragile—were deceptive. In truth, she knew well enough the reality of hard work and dedication, of personal sacrifice and self-discipline, of love and love's pain, of the sometimes almost overwhelming loneliness that invaded the life of an artist, no matter what kind. Little wonder the painter lost herself in her painting, the writer in her characters, the musician in her music. At times it was the only place to find solace.

But there was frustration as well as solace in that painting or writing or music. It was both a blessing and a burden. For the artist there were no excuses, no scapegoats. No one could step in and lend a hand when a painting wasn't going well, when characters refused to cooperate, when the tone of a piece could not be interpreted. The challenge lay in recreating what the artist saw or heard in her head. It was a continuous striving for a perfection that always seemed just out of reach.

She'd been a bit off on the Debussy sonata tonight, Taylor acknowledged to herself. The first eight or ten bars had lagged rather miserably. And it had been her fault, not the accompanist's. It seemed as though she'd been over it a hundred times before and still couldn't get it right.

A soft but insistent voice broke into her thoughts. "That's quite a storm you've got brewing there." Adam gently grazed the spot between her brows with the tip of his finger.

When she unwittingly flinched at his touch, his eyes narrowed. "I-I'm sorry, Adam. You caught me off guard," she stammered apologetically. "I guess I was off someplace. . . ."

"I guess you were," he said with a bit more tolerance. "You didn't seem to be having a very good time."

"I was thinking about some rough spots in the Debussy piece tonight," she elaborated with a sigh, not expecting him to understand.

He stopped dead in the middle of the sidewalk and firmly brought her face around to his. "Believe it or not, I do understand. You're a perfectionist, honey. If you didn't care so damned much you probably wouldn't be the great musician you are."

Her eyes widened expressively. "People outside the field usually don't understand that. They think it's merely a matter of learning the music and then playing it. Actually, it's when I'm satisfied with my own performance that I really begin to worry," she added with a short, dry laugh.

"I suppose it's all part of the creative process," Adam said, studying her for a moment or two. "And now if you've dissected your performance for tonight —which, I might add, held the audience spellbound— let's both relax and have that cup of coffee."

Taylor looked up at him with a grateful smile. "All right," she said lightly, hooking her arm through his.

The coffee shop was anything but fancy, but she scarcely noticed the decor as she slipped into the booth across from Adam. He took two plastic-coated menus from behind a bottle of ketchup and handed her one. She was about to ask him why they needed menus to order a simple cup of coffee when he glanced up at her.

"I didn't have a chance to grab any dinner before

the concert," he remarked casually. "How about you?"

Taylor met his inquiring gaze. "Yes, I had a salad earlier," she replied, thinking of the delicious concoction of crabmeat and avocado she'd made herself. She always ate simply but well. "Do you mean to tell me you came to the concert straight from your office?" she asked, her brows drawn in a thoughtful frown.

"It's more like a desk than an office," he said, grinning, "and I don't keep regular mealtimes. A policeman learns to eat on the run." Adam reached across the formica-topped table and curled his fingers around hers. "Hey, don't look so concerned. I'm not about to starve to death."

But Taylor found she was concerned and oddly touched that after a long day, this man had skipped his dinner to come hear her perform. And she had a funny feeling that when he did eat it was in second-rate coffee shops like this one. The thought made her stomach turn over.

She stole a long look at him over the top of her menu. "Do you ever cook for yourself, Adam?"

"Sure I do." He shrugged, staring off into space for a moment. "Preheat oven to 400°. Remove tray from carton. Roll foil back from chicken portion only. Bake for thirty minutes," he recited as if by rote. The look of distaste on her face must have transmitted itself to him. "It might not be exactly gourmet fare, honey, but frozen dinners are a godsend to a bachelor who's never had the wherewithal to learn how to cook," he retorted, looking down to study the menu in his hands.

Well, perhaps *he* considered frozen TV dinners a godsend, but Taylor suddenly experienced the unmistakable urge to cook a *real* meal for this man. He obviously needed someone to look after him, to care for him. Good Lord, Adam McCord was stirring maternal feelings in her! Now that was a joke! She'd never met anyone she felt less like a mother to than this big, broad-shouldered police detective. But the nagging thought persisted in the back of her mind even as the waitress appeared by the table to take their order.

Ignoring protocol, Taylor indicated that Adam's order should be taken first. "I'll have a double burger with everything. Everything but onion that is," he amended with a meaningful glance at Taylor. "A side order of French fries and a cup of black coffee."

"Just black coffee, please," Taylor told the woman when it was her turn. She slid the unused menu back behind the bottle of ketchup. "How ever do you keep your boyish figure eating food like that?" she ventured once the waitress had disappeared.

"Chasing criminals is considered very good exercise," Adam said in a teasing tone, pulling a pack of cigarettes from his breast pocket. "Do you mind if I smoke?"

Taylor shook her head to indicate that she had no objections. She did, but not on any personal grounds. She simply hated to think what cigarette smoking was doing to the lungs inside that burly chest. "What happened to the bubble gum trick?"

"I'm afraid I'm all out at the moment," he said with a faintly cynical smile. "Besides, it's been a hell of a job preparing the security for this concert. In fact, I spent most of the day on the telephone with federal authorities or out at the Civic Auditorium."

"You don't think there will be any real trouble, do you?" she remarked after due consideration.

"No, but there are certain measures that have to be taken whenever political figures are involved, foreign or domestic," he informed her in a no-nonsense voice.

"Certain measures?"

"Yes, we have to run a check on any previous or potential troublemakers in the area. We want to know where they are especially at a time like this. Then we have to map out all the entrances to the auditorium itself and assign men to cover them. Once the area is secured, we bring in the bomb squad."

"The bomb squad," Taylor repeated, trying to keep the quiver out of her voice. "Do you think that's really necessary?"

Adam gave a decisive nod of his head, his eyes never leaving hers. "It's a routine precaution in a case like this. There's nothing for you to worry about. I'm sure the whole thing will come off without a hitch." There was an odd little silence between them. "I didn't mean to say anything to upset you, Taylor. These really are routine precautions. With all the dignitaries visiting Knoxville during the six months of the World's Fair, the department got a lot of experience with this kind of thing."

She was saved from making any comment by the reappearance of the waitress with their coffee. She wasn't unduly concerned. It was simply that violence in any form was abhorrent to her. The world could be a crazy place when people allowed emotions to over-rule reason.

And hatred was the most destructive emotion of all. Hate and perhaps love. They were two sides of the same coin. Taylor had never really hated anyone in her entire life. Oh, for a while after their breakup, she had thought she hated David. But she really didn't. She was more disappointed than anything. Love—it turned out—did not automatically ensure understanding. She could look back on that episode now, after more than five years, and count herself lucky she hadn't married him. It would never have worked.

"You're scowling again," Adam pointed out, his tone coaxing, affectionate. "And from your expression, I only hope I'm not the subject of your thoughts."

"I was thinking about an old boyfriend," Taylor answered without thinking, taking a sip of her coffee.

"An old boyfriend," he echoed with an enigmatic smile. "You wound me, madame. Aren't you afraid of damaging my male ego, thinking about another man when you're with me?"

"I wouldn't say your ego is in any immediate danger," she said, smiling. "And if it will make you feel any better I was thinking how lucky I was not to have married him."

"How long ago was this?" Adam asked in a nonchalant tone, not wishing to seem to attach any importance to either the question or the answer.

"Five years ago, more or less," she said vaguely.

Adam pitched his voice low. "Is he the reason you've never married?"

"Good heavens, no!" Taylor laughed. "At least not directly. Let's just say that my lifestyle isn't exactly compatible with the matrimonial state." She stared down into her half-empty cup. "Have you ever been married?"

"No," Adam said. "And for much the same reason. It's tough being married to a cop. A lot of couples don't make it."

"Apparently, it worked for your parents and your grandparents," she ventured to guess without really knowing.

Adam frowned slightly as he folded his arms across his chest. "It was easier for them in some ways. A lot of things were easier forty and sixty years ago. One of them was being a cop, only they were respectfully called 'policemen' then. My sister's a teacher back in Pittsburgh. She tells me the same thing is true for teachers today."

"Is your sister younger than you?" Taylor wondered aloud.

"That one is. I have an older sister and a younger brother as well." He stopped talking while the waitress set the plate with his double burger and French fries in front of him. "Are you sure you won't have something?"

"Just a little more coffee," Taylor replied, smiling up at the woman.

"How about you?" Adam went on as he liberally sprinkled his potatoes with salt. "Do you have any brothers or sisters?"

"No, neither," she said with a shrug. "And don't ask me if I was lonely as a child. You really don't miss what you never had."

"From the way you're gritting your teeth, I assume you got that question a lot as a kid," he speculated, providing a mild diversion with a recalcitrant bottle of ketchup.

Taylor took the bottle from him and gave it a good

wallop with the palm of her hand. It responded immediately. "It's all in the wrist action," she explained, noting his surprise.

"Maybe you're just stronger than you look." He sounded faintly dismayed as he eyed her slender form.

"That, too," Taylor confessed, pursing her lips with satisfaction. She trimphantly returned the bottle of ketchup to him.

"How do your parents feel about your being a cellist?" Adam encouraged her to do the talking since he intended to concentrate on eating for the next few minutes.

"My mother was a concert pianist and is now a private tutor. My father is a violinist," she volunteered, her gray eyes flickering with humor.

"Gee—I wonder where you get your musical talent," he said, tongue-in-cheek. "It would seem that you, too, have followed a family tradition."

"My parents never pushed me into music, but obviously growing up in that environment was bound to be a tremendous influence. I grew up thinking that Vivaldi and Dvořák were household names. Music has been a part of my life as long as I can remember. When I showed an interest in the piano my parents were encouraging, but not insistent. Then when I was twelve I discovered the cello, and the rest is history as they say."

"Didn't you ever resent all the hours you had to spend practicing? All the things you must have missed that other kids your age were doing?" Adam inquired as he finished off the sandwich in his hands.

Her reply was low and fervent. "I was never like the other children I knew anyway. I always felt different, slightly out of place. It wasn't until some years later when I attended college at the St. Louis Conservatory of Music that I understood why."

"And what was the reason?" Adam asked in a quiet voice.

"It seems I was something of a child protégée," she said, averting her eyes. "I don't know why I'm even telling you this." Her eyes traveled reluctantly to his. "It's not something I'm usually comfortable talking about with other people."

Adam contemplated her without any change of expression. "You must have been a very special child then, just as you are a very special woman now," he stated, his voice dropping to a soft tone.

Taylor looked at him for a moment, the strain fading from her expression. "Thank you, Adam." She tossed her head to one side. "How about one last cup of coffee for the road?" she suggested, letting out a sigh.

"One for the road," he agreed, signaling their waitress.

They talked of inconsequential things then—the unusually warm weather Knoxville was having for September, the likelihood of success or failure for the University of Tennessee "Volunteers" in the upcoming football season, and their favorite foods, which ranged from Taylor's choice of escargot to Adam's steak done very rare.

"Speaking of food," he brought the subject up again as they strolled back to the parking lot. "How about having dinner with me tomorrow night?"

Taylor spread her hands out in a gesture of resignation. "I'm sorry, Adam, but I'm afraid I can't. The orchestra has a special rehearsal scheduled tomorrow night and it could go on until all hours."

His face took on an appraising look. "I see." He

paused a moment when they reached her car, his eyes hard as he gazed down at her. "Listen, Taylor, I'm not the kind of man who enjoys playing games. I want to ask you a straightforward question and I would appreciate an honest answer." He waited until she had nodded her agreement before going on. "Do you want to see me again?"

She blinked, stood back and took in a long, slow breath. A slight breeze rolled a crisp brown leaf along the pavement. "Yes," she said, somehow feeling she had sealed her fate with that single word. "I want to see you again."

Adam did not bother to disguise his pleasure. "Then it's only a matter of deciding on the time and place, isn't it? How about my place after the concert next week? I'll supply the steaks if you'll agree to supervise their grilling. I don't think I'm quite up to snails just yet," he added with an amused chuckle.

Taylor faced him, smiling, but quite serious. "All right, we'll have dinner at your place Thursday after the concert." After all, Taylor reminded herself, she was a mature woman. She didn't need anyone's permission to go to this man's apartment. But a small inner voice insisted on also reminding her that she barely knew Adam McCord. "I'll bring the dessert," she heard herself offer. "You do like cheesecake, don't you?"

Adam was slow to reply. "Cheesecake?" he repeated in a vague tone, leaning his hand on the car behind her. "Yes, I like cheesecake."

Taylor suddenly stood there very still, realizing that if she turned her head even the smallest fraction, her face would be buried in the sleeve of his jacket. The parking lot seemed shrouded in intimate shadows she hadn't noticed before. The light cast by the lamp on the corner was more than effectively blocked out by the broad-shouldered man looming over her.

She felt surrounded by his presence, by the scent that clung to him, a subtle mixture of his natural maleness and the aroma of coffee and cigarettes. His breath was even warmer than the September breeze that teased the tendrils about her face. Unsteadily, her heart began to pick up speed.

She stirred uneasily. "Adam—"

"Shhhh—" He touched the tip of his finger to her lips.

Then he propped his other hand against the car and she was trapped between the cool metal and the warmth of his body, a warmth that seemed to beckon her closer to its source. She was intensely aware of his vibrant form, the long line of his thighs an inch away from hers, the heat emanating through the material of his shirt. She sensed rather than felt an imperceptible movement on his part. Then his lips skimmed her forehead in a feathery light caress. She heard a sharp little intake of air and knew it was her own. Her instinctive reaction was to look up; when she did, Taylor found him waiting there for her.

Adam's eyes appeared to be closed, but she could feel him watching her. His face was so close she could make out the tiny lines at the corners of his mouth even in the dark. She reached out, intending to push him away, but when she encountered his shirt and the muscled wall of his chest beneath, all her intentions were forgotten. She felt the strong, rhythmic beat of his heart under her hand in the fraction of a second it took for his mouth to travel the last distance to hers.

The touch of him was surprisingly smooth and soft

as his lips grazed hers in the merest hint of a kiss. He seemed to inhale the sweet scent of her breath into his lungs. She unconsciously moistened her lips at the same instant his mouth enclosed hers. A slight tremor ran through them both at the unexpected intimacy. The tip of her tongue encountered his teeth and was trapped there by the heat of their kiss.

With a groan that started in the back of his throat, Adam opened his mouth wider and drew her into him. His tongue darted back and forth in a little mating dance before plunging deeper to drink of her sweetness. His body shifted until Taylor was half-supporting him, her back pressed against the cold metal, her hand flattened between them, her breasts crushed beneath the impact of his weight.

Everything about him was overwhelming—the nearness of his taut body, the mastery of his kiss, the taste of his mouth on hers. She was no longer in control of the situation, or of herself for that matter. In the space of a few short minutes her relationship with this man had metamorphosed into something she could not explain and did not understand.

And then it ended as abruptly as it had begun. Adam tore his mouth from hers, his chest rapidly rising and falling in what seemed an almost painful quest for air. He eased his weight from her and leaned against the car for support. After a moment, he raised his head and looked her in the eyes.

"Damn!" he swore under his breath; the hand he raked through his hair was shaking ever so slightly. "I honestly didn't mean for that to happen."

"Neither did I." She laughed softly, a laugh that belied the tremors still shooting through her body.

His hand came up to cup her chin. "I never planned

for it to be any more than a proper good-night kiss," he said apologetically.

Taylor reached up and placed her hand over his. "It's all right, Adam. Really, it is. Sometimes these things just happen." Who was she kidding? These *things* didn't just happen to her. She had too much self-discipline to lose control simply because a man kissed her.

"I guess it's getting late," he said after the briefest of pauses.

"Yes, it is," Taylor agreed, wondering if it could truly be uncertainty she saw in his eyes.

"A late dinner on Thursday then?" Adam reiterated, reaching around to open the car door for her.

Did he half-expect her to have changed her mind? Common sense dictated that that was exactly what she should do. "I'll see you after the concert," she said instead.

"Good night, Taylor," he murmured, bending his head to brush his lips across hers in a thoroughly proper kiss.

"Good night, Adam," she returned, pausing by the open door. "Do you *really* like cheesecake?" she asked at the last minute.

"Yes, I really do." He laughed, shutting the car door after her.

As she slipped into bed a half-hour later, she remembered the vow she had made earlier that evening never to see Adam McCord again. She had told herself then that he would just have to get his laughs someplace else.

Well, Taylor thought to herself as she drifted off to sleep, it seemed the laugh was on her.

3

It was an evening of excellence. An evening of Brahms and Beethoven and Mozart. An evening of unexcelled listening pleasure for those in the audience and a triumph from the first note to the last for the Knoxville Symphony Orchestra.

At a time when even major symphony orchestras around the country were battling for financial survival, when budgets were being cut and ticket sales declining along with government subsidies, this was an evening that reaffirmed the invaluable worth of symphonic music. For the Knoxville Symphony it was an event equaled only by the concert given in conjunction with the University of Tennessee when they presented famed violinist Itzhak Perlman in recital.

When the final note of the encore was played the conductor and concertmaster and the eighty-odd members of the orchestra took their deserved bows.

The visiting ambassador and his American hosts were the first to take their leave, and then the Civic Auditorium began to empty quickly.

The commotion backstage was understandable. Nervous tension always ran high before a concert of this magnitude and the resulting release of energy was noisy, sometimes explosive. Everyone seemed to be talking at once as they congratulated each other on a job well done.

Taylor stood there in her long black dress, its color and style emphasizing her slender figure and the high, full swell of her breasts. Her hair was swept up in a sophisticated chignon for the evening's performance. The members of the orchestra were dressed in formal attire tonight, but some of the men had already undone their ties and taken off their jackets.

Taylor Jameson always enjoyed this feeling of camaraderie that lingered just after a concert. A camaraderie that bound this diverse group of men and women together in a single purpose—to perform, not as individuals, but as a unified whole. It was this sense of common purpose she had missed during her travels as a solo performer.

It was the same sense of common purpose, of mutual understanding, that drove her to teach at the University. It was a thrill quite unlike any other to have talented students in her seminars, knowing what might lie ahead for them. To think that one of them could be the next Pablo Casals or Rostropovich or Janos Starker. To think that she might be the catalyst, the mentor of that kind of rare talent.

No one understood better than Taylor the triumph and the loneliness of possessing a unique gift. She knew firsthand of the constant striving that was necessary to reach the highest levels of virtuosity. In the end, the music had to be its own reward. That was the secret she wanted to share with others like herself. Fame and attention were fleeting, transitory; satisfaction from *within* lasted a lifetime.

But tonight there was no loneliness, only the glorious euphoria and triumph they shared as a group. Taylor was chatting with several other members of the fifty-five-piece string section when Paul Harrell came up and slipped a casual arm about her shoulders.

She had dated the dashing violinist several times in the past year until she discovered that the one thing bigger than Paul Harrell's six-foot frame was his ego. He was admittedly handsome with his blond, sophisticated good looks and he knew it. His charm was legendary, his women were presumably legion.

"Taylor, you're looking lovelier than ever," he drawled with theatrical intimacy. "A group is going to Piccolo's for a celebration drink. Why don't you join us?"

"Oh, I'd love to, Paul, but I have a prior commitment," she murmured ruefully, swallowing the laughter that lurked at the back of her throat. It would never do for Paul to find out she considered him hilariously funny. He wouldn't think it was funny at all. "Perhaps another time," Taylor added in a wistful voice.

"Speaking of prior commitments—" Andrea Martin joined the circle, her statuesque figure even more striking in the plain black she wore to perfection—"I think I spotted yours over there, Taylor." She nonchalantly glanced over her shoulder as she spoke. "And do remember what I've always said— " the woman paused for emphasis—"it's dangerous taking the *law* into your own hands."

Refusing to give Andrea the satisfaction of seeing her blush, Taylor looked coolly past her and saw Adam waiting in the wings. He was an imposing figure standing there in the shadows, tall and dark. He appeared confident, watchful, despite the bustle of activity going on around him. She'd noticed before this apparent ability of his to stand back and quietly observe the rest of them. It was disconcerting at times.

How strange, Taylor thought, her gaze returning to the man beside her. The two men were of nearly equal size and stature and yet, no one would seriously consider Paul Harrell a threat. There was something inherently dangerous in Adam, a fundamental maleness that was at once subtle and undeniable. Andrea Martin recognized it as surely as she did herself. A woman would.

And she knew the moment Adam spotted her. His tanned face underwent that miraculous transformation she was already learning to look for, to expect from him. Taylor suddenly realized it made Adam McCord doubly dangerous. He could disarm even the staunchest foe with that dazzling smile of his.

"Excuse me," Taylor murmured to no one in particular, as she turned and walked toward that smile.

"Hello, Taylor," he said silkily, meeting her halfway.

"Hello, Adam," she greeted him with what she hoped was a casual air.

"I must say you people put on quite a show," Adam drawled, looking her over from head to toe at his leisure. "And you're even more stunning in black than I remembered," he added in a husky voice, then blinked as if realizing for the first time just how openly he was staring at her.

"Thank you," Taylor rasped, half afraid the man

might well intend to eat her up and swallow her whole. "Did you get to hear any of the concert?" she stammered, more for something to say than anything.

"I heard a little of it," he told her truthfully, "but my mind was obviously on other things than music tonight. With our distinguished visitors now in the capable hands of federal authorities, I feel like I can relax for the first time in a week," Adam admitted, breathing a sigh of relief.

"Are you sure you still want to have dinner tonight?" she asked in her softest tone, noting the smudges under his eyes and the deep furrows marring his brow. She could have sworn they weren't there the last time she saw him.

"Why? Have you changed your mind?" His voice was quiet, dangerously quiet to her way of thinking.

"No, I haven't changed my mind," she replied. "But it is late, Adam, and you look tired."

"Perhaps the truth is you would prefer to join your *friend* for a drink," he suggested, a hint of sarcasm creeping into his tone. It was almost as if he had eavesdropped on her conversation with Paul Harrell. But that was impossible, of course.

"My *friends* frequently go out for a drink after a concert," Taylor icily informed him. "I was well aware of that fact when I accepted your invitation."

"I see. . . ." Adam said in a soft voice, but his expression bore no trace of apology. "Well, that's good." He nodded briskly, his frown once again becoming a smile. "Because I had one heck of a time shopping for just the right steaks for tonight." But it was something akin to relief that Taylor saw flicker in his eyes.

She glanced down at the formal black gown she was wearing and then back at Adam. "I brought a pair of slacks with me. Would you mind waiting while I change?"

"No, I don't mind waiting. In fact, if you tell me where your stuff is I'll put it in the car while you get dressed," he offered, looking around as though he half-expected to be able to pick her cello out from all the other instruments backstage. "Oh, by the way, I hope you don't mind," Adam said, bringing his eyes back to hers. "I didn't drive my car tonight. I rode over with one of the other officers."

"I guess there's no sense in both of us driving if we don't have to," Taylor said with a shrug. "My things are over there and you'll need my car keys, of course." She took the key chain from her handbag and neatly dropped it in his outstretched palm. "Be sure not to set anything on the box in the back seat," she added as an afterthought. "If you do you'll crush our dessert."

"Yes, ma'am," he drawled with what sounded suspiciously like a chuckle. "And I wouldn't want to do that, now would I?"

"I'll have you know, Adam McCord, that I spent most of the afternoon making that lousy cheesecake," Taylor retorted, the snap back in her voice.

"Then I promise I'll be doubly careful, honey," he intoned, reaching out to lazily brush his fingertips across her bottom lip. It was as underhanded a way to shut a woman up as any she'd ever seen. The man didn't play fair. "I'll be back in a few minutes," Adam said, turning to collect her things.

Making disparaging little sounds under her breath,

Taylor stomped off to the ladies' room. She'd left her slacks and shirt in a locker there before the concert. It was a simple matter of slipping out of her dress and slip and into the tailored pants and coordinated silk blouse. They were both a shade of periwinkle that brought out the blue in her eyes.

Her black dress shoes were replaced with a pair of casual, low-heeled sandals. She wasn't about to stand around grilling steaks at eleven o'clock at night in three-inch heels! Of course, the disadvantage was losing those three inches when it came to standing up to Adam McCord.

Taylor took another minute to check her makeup in the mirror above the sink, deciding at the last minute that her chignon looked rather silly now that she was dressed in casual clothes. She quickly removed the hairpins that held it in place and gave her head a good shake. A few brisk strokes with a brush and she was ready. Stuffing the lacy slip into her handbag, she tossed the black dress over her arm, picked up the pair of discarded heels and opened the door.

Adam was nonchalantly leaning with his back against the wall outside the ladies' room. He pushed himself into an upright stance as he saw her emerge, her hands full.

"Here—let me help you with that," he volunteered, taking the shoes from her and partially freeing one of her hands in the process.

"You look ridiculous carrying a pair of women's high heels," Taylor needlessly pointed out. Would he look any less ridiculous carrying her dress or, God forbid, her handbag?

"I really don't think there is a dignified way out of

this," he replied with uncustomary seriousness. "If I let you carry it all while I walk out empty-handed, then I look like a number one *heel,* if you'll pardon the pun. It's a case of damned if I do and damned if I don't."

"You should have held on to that cello case a little longer," Taylor shot back with a grin.

She saw a flash of white teeth. "Aren't you concerned about how this is going to look to your friends?" Adam purred with more than a touch of innuendo.

"They could care less if your preference is to wear women's shoes," she countered in a flippant tone. "They're very liberal-minded when it comes to that sort of thing."

"I'd watch it if I were you, my dear Taylor," he softly growled close to her ear, his arm enclosing her shoulders. "When push comes to shove you're way out of your league."

"Well, we'll just have to see about that, won't we?" she said with a challenging lift of her chin. It was only a matter of minutes before they reached the station wagon. "My keys, please," Taylor requested, extending her hand.

Adam handed them over without a word and proceeded to watch as she unlocked the tailgate. Taylor practically threw her dress in the back before going around to unlock the door on the driver's side. She slipped behind the wheel and reached across to raise the lock on the passenger's door. She intended to beat a hasty retreat, but it turned out that Adam moved even quicker. He had the door open and was in the car before she could safely ensconce herself behind the steering wheel.

"I thought black was your color," he murmured, delaying her retreat, "but I was wrong. Blue is."

Taylor nervously moistened her lips and pulled away. "You'll have to give me directions to your place," she prompted, inserting the key in the ignition. The engine instantly sprang into life.

"Head for the downtown area," Adam instructed, settling back in his seat. "I'll tell you where to go from there."

She would like nothing better than to tell this man where *he* could go, but common sense prevailed as she pulled out into traffic.

She had always thought of herself as an excellent driver, but with Adam McCord comfortably sprawled beside her in the front seat Taylor found that her ability to concentrate was sorely put to the test. She felt an alarming awareness of the man sitting beside her. She knew precisely where his thigh was in relationship to her own. She sensed his slightest movement in some sixth-sense sort of way. She could even have testified in court as to the exact moment he slid his arm along the back of the seat to hover above her shoulder.

Damn him! Hadn't he ever heard of highway safety? Didn't he know of the dangers of distracting the driver? Why couldn't he simply keep his distance anyway?

Taylor felt something stir the hair about her neck and then the touch of skin against skin as Adam drew lazy little circles just below her ear with his thumb. What was he trying to do? Get them both killed? She slammed on the brakes just as the light overhead turned bright red.

"Don't do that," she hissed at him, her eyes shooting hot, angry sparks in his direction.

"Don't do *what?*" Adam inquired with childlike innocence.

Taylor shifted resentfully in her seat. "I don't want you to touch me," she softly commanded.

She felt him assessing her. "Don't you like to be touched?" He sounded surprised.

"There's a time and place for everything," she said in a prim voice.

"And you're telling me this isn't the time or place, is that it?" There was a small, mocking smile on his lips.

"Not if you want to get home in one piece tonight," she retorted, pressing her foot down on the accelerator. The station wagon shot forward in response.

Her admission seemed to please Adam McCord no end. After that he was content to sit back and look out the window, only turning to her when it was necessary to give directions.

"Turn left at the next corner," he said at last. "That's my building over there. You can park behind my car," he added, pointing it out to her.

Taylor pulled into the parking space behind his gray sedan and heaved a sigh of relief as she turned off the ignition. In her opinion, it was a miracle they'd made it without an accident. Perhaps this wasn't such a great idea after all. The truth was that Adam seemed to have some strange effect on her that she was at a loss to explain. Well, she had no intention of getting involved with him. He wasn't her type—not in the least.

"Aren't you coming in?" Adam asked, leaning against the door frame to peer down at her.

"Of course I am," she returned ungraciously. "I'll just get the cheesecake." She leaned over the back of the seat to secure the box with their dessert.

It was a fairly new apartment complex with a cluster

of four-story buildings and very little lawn. They walked up to the entrance of the nearest building and down a short hallway to the elevators.

"My apartment is on the fourth floor," he told her, pressing the button to start their ascent.

She was taken aback for a moment. "Now how did you know I was about to ask you that?"

Adam turned to her with an ear-to-ear grin. "Would you believe a piece of brilliant deductive reasoning on my part?"

Taylor bit her lip against a smile. "No, I wouldn't." She didn't realize she was holding her breath until the elevator doors slid open and Adam stepped back to allow her to precede him into a small foyer. "Have you lived here long?" she asked as he fished around in his pocket for the key.

"Since the place opened almost two years ago," he said, pushing the apartment door ajar and reaching around the corner to switch on a light.

Taylor's first reaction was one of utter surprise. Adam's apartment was nicer than she'd expected—at least she assumed it was, under all the clutter! There were books and magazines and newspapers everywhere.

The living room was dominated by a large window directly in front of her. The room was decorated in several shades of rather masculine brown, the furniture predominantly leather or perhaps its synthetic equivalent. There was an oversized desk in one corner that seemed buried in an avalanche of papers and even more books. It certainly had that lived-in look, Taylor thought to herself.

"I'm afraid I've been so busy this week I haven't had much time to clean the place up," Adam ex-

plained, snatching up a handful of newspapers from
one of the chairs. Taylor nearly laughed out loud when
he opened a closet door and indiscriminately stuffed
them inside. "C'mon," he urged, shrugging off his
jacket, "we'll have a drink in the kitchen while I put
the steaks on to cook. I don't know about you, but I'm
starved."

"The cheesecake really should be put in the refrigerator anyway," she mumbled, trailing along behind
him. "Adam, do you have a roommate?" she asked,
suddenly aware of music playing somewhere in the
apartment.

"I suppose you could say so," he said over his
shoulder.

"*Suppose?* You mean you don't know for sure?"
She laughed, tossing her handbag in a chair as she
went by.

"You'll know what I mean when I introduce you,"
Adam declared, disappearing into the kitchen. Wondering about the man's sanity, she shook her head
and followed in his footsteps. "Taylor, I'd like you to
meet Rocky."

At the sound of his voice, Taylor's head came up
with a jerk. She opened her mouth and closed it again
without speaking. On the second try she managed to
regain her voice. "Do you mean to tell me that Rocky
is a parakeet?" she exclaimed, finding herself eye to
eye with a small, yellow-and-aqua bird.

"I believe the correct term is parakeet-budgie,"
Adam said with a perfectly straight face. "I leave the
radio playing to keep him company while I'm at
work," he explained, opening the door of the wire
cage.

"I don't think I believe this," Taylor muttered under

her breath, watching as the small, plump bird hopped out of the cage and perched on the door.

"The fridge is right over there," Adam pointed out as if there were nothing out of the ordinary about a large, burly policeman having a small bird for a pet.

"How long have you and Rocky been together now?" she inquired skeptically, opening the door of the refrigerator to place the cheesecake inside.

Adam looked thoughtful for a moment. "I guess since I moved in here two years ago. He was a housewarming gift."

"Someone gave you a bird as a housewarming gift?" she queried, arching a brow.

"My sister. You know, the one who's a teacher in Pittsburgh," Adam said matter-of-factly, pushing past Taylor to retrieve the steaks from the refrigerator.

"Rocky—" She tapped her finger thoughtfully against her bottom lip. "I assume he's named for the Rockefellers."

That brought a laugh from Adam. "He's named for Rocky Marciano."

She knitted her brows together. "Who?"

"Rocky Marciano," he carefully enunciated, "the heavyweight boxing champion."

"Oh—*that* Marciano!" she mocked in a tone reminiscent of one he'd once used with her.

Adam turned and gently pinned her against the refrigerator door. "Touché, honey. I see you haven't forgotten that night any more than I have." He brought his mouth down to within a fraction of hers, his breath wafting warm and sweet against her face.

"Adam—" Taylor's voice sank to a caressing murmur, "I think your bird just crashed."

The sensual haze clouding his eyes immediately

cleared, replaced by practical concern. "Don't move!" he ordered, cautiously turning around. Actually, she'd had no intention of moving. "I wouldn't want you to step on him." He did a fair imitation of tiptoeing across the kitchen, despite the fact that his shoe size had to be at least an eleven.

"You mean Rocky doesn't fly?" She felt ridiculous even asking the question.

Adam carefully approached the diminutive form crouched on the floor beneath the bird cage. "Not very well, I'm afraid. It's French molt."

"French molt? I assume that's not a social disease," she said, concealing a smile.

"No, and it's not a salad dressing either. It's a vitamin deficiency or something. Anyway, Rocky lost his large wing and tail feathers about six months ago. Since then he's been more or less reduced to walking."

"Do they have such a thing as vitamin supplements for birds?"

The man gently picked the parakeet up and returned him to the cage. "As a matter of fact, they do. I take Rocky to the vet's for a shot of vitamins and cortisone every couple of weeks."

"How in the world do they give a little bird like that a shot?" Taylor asked, suddenly finding her sympathies were with Rocky. "And don't tell me *very carefully.*"

His eyebrows rose fractionally. "Well, it isn't easy. If you think I look funny handling Rocky, you should see the veterinarian. The guy is six foot six if he's an inch."

"Two great big men against one poor little bird," she crooned, peering into the cage. Good grief, Taylor thought, it had finally come to this. She was talking to a bird! The parakeet immediately hopped toward her and began to chatter. "Does he talk?" She could have sworn she recognized several human words amidst the bird's chatter.

"Some birds have the ability to imitate the human voice. Of course, they don't understand what they're saying." As if to prove his point, the bird let out with an exaggerated wolf whistle. "Well, not usually, anyway. In this case, I couldn't agree with him more," Adam drawled with a slightly wicked grin. He snapped the cage door shut. "Sorry about that, Rocky, but two's company, three's a crowd." He turned to Taylor and spoke in a brisk, businesslike tone. "What can you do with some tomatoes and lettuce? I thought we'd have a salad with our steaks."

"If you'll allow me to rummage around in your refrigerator I'll see what I can come up with."

While Adam prepared the broiler pan with their steaks, Taylor located several tomatoes, a head of lettuce and a bottle of Italian salad dressing. She carefully washed and cored the tomatoes, expertly sliced them into eighths and placed them in a shallow bowl. Then she sprinkled on enough salad dressing to cover them.

Placing a glass of red wine on the counter in front of her, Adam watched her work. "Why do I get the feeling you've done this before?" he speculated with equal amounts of admiration and amusement.

"Probably because I have," she said dryly, taking a sip of her wine. "Hmmm . . . that's quite good. Normally, I make my own dressing with olive oil and vinegar and spices. And you're supposed to marinate the tomatoes for several hours in the refrigerator. I'm afraid this is a rather poor imitation of the original recipe."

"What's it called?" he asked curiously, taking two plates from the cupboard above her head.

"Tomatoes vinaigrette," she said, arranging a lettuce leaf on each place before draining and adding the tomatoes.

"Funny," Adam said, looking intrigued, "but I never thought of you as the domestic type."

"I'm not certain I know what you mean by the domestic type," she countered with an irritated flicker of her gray eyes. "I enjoy cooking if that's what you mean, but then so do a lot of men. Does that make them the domestic type?"

He cleared his throat uncomfortably. "I, ah, better check on our steaks," he coughed, choking back his laughter. "I wouldn't want to burn them."

"I thought you said you couldn't cook," Taylor was saying some twenty minutes later as she savored the last bite of her steak. "That was delicious."

"Thank you. I'm glad you enjoyed it." Adam accepted the compliment as though it were only his due. "Are you ready for dessert?"

She emphatically shook her head from side to side. "I couldn't eat another bite right now, but I'd be glad to cut you a piece of cheesecake."

"Tell you what," he said, reaching across the table to enfold her hand in his, "why don't you take your wine into the other room while I rinse the dishes? You could put some music on if you like. It'll only take me a minute to clean up here."

"All right, if you prefer." She was feeling particularly amenable after two glasses of wine and a full dinner at this late hour. With her glass in hand, Taylor rose from the table and made what she hoped was a graceful exit.

Perhaps under other circumstances the sight of the cluttered room would have made her hands itch to straighten it, but tonight she contented herself with merely cleaning some of the debris off the sofa. She was about to curl up in one corner with her glass of wine when she remembered Adam's suggestion to put some music on.

It took several minutes to locate the tape player amidst the magazines and books stacked on the shelves behind his desk. She studied his collection of cassettes for some time before choosing one she hoped was soft and soothing in keeping with her mood. She flipped the cassette into the player and stood there listening as the mellow sounds of a popular male singer filled the room.

Instead of returning to her place on the sofa, Taylor found her attention drawn to the bookshelves in front of her. She took another sip of wine as she lightly ran her fingers along the row of titles: *Modern Criminal Procedures, Criminal Law Digest, Scientific Evidence in Criminal Cases, Searches and Seizures, Arrests and Confessions*. Adam certainly had a lot of law books! At first, it didn't strike her as odd. After all, he was a police detective. But surely not every policeman kept a library of law volumes. She would have to remember to ask him about it when he was finished in the kitchen.

Then she discovered, much to her delight, a shelf of mystery and suspense novels. This was definitely more her taste, Taylor decided, thinking of her own penchant for Dorothy L. Sayers and Ngaio Marsh.

Apparently, Adam's tastes in the genre ran more to the realistic American writers than the tidy British aristocrats she favored herself. She noticed he seemed to have a complete collection of Dashiell Hammett detective novels.

Taylor took the first volume down and thumbed through it. She'd seen the movie version of "The Maltese Falcon," of course, but she had never actually read Hammett's novel. She had always been more than a little fascinated by the mind that could create such memorable characters as Sam Spade or Nick Charles in *The Thin Man*. She flipped back to the beginning of the book, intending to read just a page or two, but found herself reading on.

"Are you a Dashiell Hammett fan?" The deep, husky voice came from behind her.

Taylor whirled around to see Adam standing in the doorway between the living room and kitchen. With his tie off and the first several buttons of his shirt undone, he suddenly, frighteningly looked all male. His sleeves were rolled up to his elbows and she could see the soft, dark hair on his forearms. There was a promise of great strength in those arms and in the expanse of his broad chest. The clean, taut lines of his waist and thighs seemed to hold a promise of their own. There was no denying the presence of the man, the sense of subtle danger that radiated from him.

"I-I suppose like most people I've seen the movie versions of Hammett's novels on the late show," she stammered, moistening her bottom lip. "I've never actually *read* any of his books."

"He only wrote five, you know," Adam informed her in a conversational tone. "What a hell of a waste," he swore softly. "The man's later years were spent in ill health and a myriad of other problems. He was something of a mentor to playwright and author Lillian Hellman for decades, but he never wrote another novel after *The Thin Man* in 1934. You're welcome to take the book home with you if you like," he added as an afterthought.

"Thank you," Taylor mumbled, snapping the book closed. "I think I will."

"How about a refill?" Without waiting for an answer, Adam took the glass from her hand and disappeared into the kitchen again. He reemerged several minutes later with two freshly filled wineglasses.

Taylor graciously accepted the one he held out to her before moving to the sofa. She curled up in one corner, sipping the dry red wine, aware of Adam as he sat down beside her and casually stretched his long legs out under the coffee table in front of them. He put his head back against the leather sofa and closed his eyes.

"This is nice." His voice sounded quiet and slow. "I've been looking forward to this night for the past week." Adam turned his head to one side and studied her through hooded eyelids.

"So have I," she admitted in a half-whisper, nervously clutching the stem of her wineglass. Her movements suddenly stilled as a large, warm hand reached out to lightly touch a long, blond strand of hair draped across her shoulder.

"You have beautiful hair," he rumbled softly, his other hand reaching out to take the glass from hers and set it on the coffee table.

"Adam—" Her voice broke for a second. "It's getting late." She had known all evening that this moment would arrive, that he would kiss her again.

She'd been afraid to ask herself what the inevitable outcome would be. Now the time had come and she was no closer to an answer.

"Oh, Taylor," he whispered, burying his lips in her hair, "I could make such a fool of myself over you."

Taylor let out a small sigh. She somehow had serious doubts about that. Adam McCord was no man's or woman's fool. "I bet you say that to all the girls." Her faint smile flickered and died. It was an uneasy attempt at humor that had fallen completely flat. There was something disturbing about this man, something that made her want to take up arms and defend herself.

"I told you before, honey, I don't play games." An edge of steel underlined Adam's velvety soft voice.

The truth of his claim was brought home to her as he lowered his head and found her mouth with stunning accuracy. The wine had become all the sweeter on his lips; the taste of him was heady, intoxicating, drugging to her senses. If someone were going to be made a fool of she knew instinctively who it would be. Perhaps she could talk herself into believing that Adam wasn't her type, but his brand of kisses most assuredly was.

With a leisurely grace, his mouth moved over hers, exploring, savoring, but not demanding. He seemed content to linger over the smallest nuance of response she gave him, to discover for himself all there was to learn about her wine-sweetened kiss. She was stunned to find there was so very much for him to learn. He retreated a breath away, his fingertip tracing the little valley that dipped at the center of her upper lip, sensitizing the tender flesh, sending a tiny earthquake shuddering along her nerve endings. Then the tip of his tongue joined in the gentle, sensuous search and of its own accord her mouth opened invitingly.

It was an invitation Adam seemed to find impossible to refuse. He was suddenly an integral part of her, melting into her so that two mouths became one, their breath intermingled, their desire of singular purpose. She was suddenly desperate for his kiss, for his touch, just as surely as he was for hers. Her mouth opened wider, wanting more of him, unknowingly giving more of herself in the process.

It was no longer important to think, only to feel. It no longer mattered which of them was the fool as they rushed in where wisdom had already lost its foothold. Together they crossed the fine line that divided sanity from madness, and found that madness could indeed be sweet.

"So incredibly sweet," Adam murmured in a husky voice, drinking of her warmth, taking it into himself and returning it with a fiery heat of his own.

Taylor felt him reach out for her and knew in that instant she would eagerly, willingly go into his arms. "Hold me, Adam," she heard an oddly breathless voice implore.

"I will," he assured her. "I will!"

4

And he did.

With a passionate reverence he gathered her up in his arms, drawing her closer and closer to the incendiary heat of his body. He was so very big and strong. Taylor found herself glorying in that fact as she was boldly anchored against his male form. Her hands reached out to entwine themselves about his neck, to experience for the first time the feel of her fingers in the thick hair that brushed his shirt collar, to wonder at its softness. She marveled at this contradiction in a man who seemed so hard in every other way.

Yet she was not the only one to discover an apparent contradiction.

"So cool on the outside, so warm underneath," Adam murmured hoarsely, running his hands in a light caressing motion over her silk blouse and up to the vulnerable skin at her nape. He threaded his fingers through the mass of her ash-blond hair, using a fistful as a silken cord to bring her to him once more.

This time there was no hesitation as their lips met in a searing kiss—a kiss that left its brand on them both. Long, strong fingers gently but firmly held her face up to his, covering the pulse at the base of her throat, tracing the vee of her blouse where it plunged downward toward the swell of her breasts. His hand slid inside her collar to find the enticing warmth of a bare shoulder, the defined outline of a delicate bone. His touch was hot and slightly rough as it grazed the softness of her skin. And she shivered in spite of herself.

Oh, dear God, Taylor thought desperately, this was crazy! She didn't want to want him. Her life was nicely planned and under control. There was simply no place in it for the disruptive influence of this man, or any man for that matter. But even as the thought passed through her mind, she felt the velvety insistence of his tongue, robbing her of both breath and conviction in the same instant.

Somewhere through the web of sensuality that Adam wove so well Taylor became aware of her own hands seeking to know him beneath the opening of his shirt, finding his flesh and muscle arousing not only her awareness of him, but of herself as well.

It had been so long since she had touched another human being in this way—perhaps as never before. She didn't want to discover the excitement, the passion she could arouse in him or he in her. She had to be sufficient unto herself. Most of all, she did not want to become vulnerable. She must not grow to need this man's kiss, this man's touch as one of life's necessities. He was a luxury she simply couldn't afford.

If he had given her a moment's respite perhaps she might have found the strength to pull away, but there was no such relief to be found in Adam's embrace. Just as she thought to end the intimacy between them, his hand glided down to gently cup her breast.

She clutched at his shirt. "Adam—"

"I love the way you smell, the way you feel," he rasped, his mouth effectively silencing hers.

Taylor felt her stomach flip over in a somersault, heard a low, sensuous moan issue from her lips, felt his hand rock back and forth, gently massaging the nipple that peaked through the silky material of her shirt to tease his palm. At her response, his kiss deepened. She felt as though he were devouring her as his tongue plunged in to raid the honeyed sweetness of her mouth.

"Oh, God, Taylor, I could almost break you in two!" Adam growled, his fingers lightly encircling her throat. "I know I should keep my hands off you, but to feel you respond like that to my touch . . ." With a groan that bordered on anguish, he sought to obliterate all thought by grinding his mouth down on hers with a passion that was at once frightening and soul-shattering.

She found herself responding to him as she had never dreamt herself capable of responding to any man. It shattered every preconceived notion she had of passion between a man and a woman. This was no lukewarm emotion, but a white-hot flame that burned out of control. This took over the mind and body and even the soul. There was no dignity in it, no room for pride or self-discipline. It turned Taylor's world upside down and inside out for a moment.

Now she understood the true nature of the danger

she had sensed in this man. Her life was one of order and discipline. There was nothing ordered about passion. That was an indisputable fact and one well worth remembering.

Yet she found herself unable to resist the desire that flowed back and forth between them, taking from one to give to the other, gaining strength from their mutual weakness, growing into a force with a mind of its own. There was no longer any doubt that Adam wanted her. The question was did she want him?

That question was answered for her as Adam lifted her in his arms and settled her across his lap. Lured by the strength and need that emanated from him, she raised not a word of protest. Instead, her arms reached out to encompass him, finding the attempt futile because of his size.

He seemed determined to show her that the electricity that flowed between them was as much her doing as his. His teeth and lips nibbled on the soft flesh of her ear, the tender juncture of neck and shoulder, the proud jut of her chin as it buried itself in his collar. His touch moved in erotic prologue over her body, discovering a symphony of delights, a myriad of passionate tones buried just below the surface.

Taylor began a journey of her own with no thought for the final destination. In a light caress, she ran her fingertips across the snowy-white material of his shirt, inadvertently stroking the mat of dark hair beneath, the hard, aroused male nipples. With an odd sense of female delight she felt a shudder rack his body. Her hands moved over him with the same strong sensitivity she brought to her music.

It was a dream come true for Adam—to feel her

hands on him as he had once only imagined. "Oh, honey, don't stop now," he pleaded in a voice thick with heightened passion.

Something in her wanted to grant his wish, to respond to the male urgency in his request. The power he allowed her to wield over him proved to be heady indeed. It tapped something fundamental that had lain dormant in her through the years. Taylor suddenly found herself wanting to give pleasure as well as to receive it.

She rained little kisses over his face and neck, kisses that teased and provoked, kisses that promised far more than they delivered. It nearly drove Adam to the brink of madness. Yet he submitted to her will, knowing that to do so now would bring them both greater pleasure in the end.

When he could stand it no longer Adam turned her gently in his arms, and in one fluid motion she was stretched out on the sofa as he eased himself down beside her. Her back was pressed into the warm leather. Her hands were trapped between her own quivering form and the unyielding hardness of his.

She gazed up into his face, reading there the need that drove him, seeing the desire that burned brightly in his dark eyes, noting the sensuous twist to his mouth before it was lowered to her throat. Stinging kisses were showered on her skin, kisses that were temptation itself.

Taylor felt herself instinctively yielding to that temptation, throwing her head back to reveal even more of her soft, white throat to his caress. Her head moved from side to side in mindless wonder. Small whimpers of unspoken desire bubbled to the surface, slipping past her parted lips as he slowly undid her blouse one button at a time. His gaze was riveted to her passion-ridden features as the silky material finally gave way.

The bit of lacy bra was gently pushed aside, her breasts freed. She was first aware of his breath scorching her bare flesh and then the tentative touch of his hand.

"Adam—" His name was on her lips as his fingers found the swell of her breast, moving over her in a mere whisper of a caress. Tantalizingly, he captured the tender tip and traced an erotic pattern back and forth across its sensitized surface.

"You're beautiful," Adam muttered in a strangely husky voice. "More beautiful than I ever imagined." He watched as she eagerly grew to fill his hand, marveling at the passion his touch could elicit from her. Her nipples hardened in almost painful arousal, seeming to beg for the physical release only he could give.

That release came as he found her first with the tip of his arrowed tongue and then with lips that seemed to hunger for her. He nipped at the taut peak with his teeth; his tongue erotically darted back and forth, driving her to arch against him. Her breast was plunged even deeper into his mouth, creating a kind of frenzied madness in them both.

A path of searing heat was trailed across her flesh as his mouth wandered from one breast down to her soft belly and back up to the other. He took small, delicious nibbles along the way, tasting every inch of her for himself. She was obviously to his liking. He paused at last to linger over one rosy bud, gently tugging at it, rolling his tongue around it in a lazy circle until Taylor was quite sure it was both heaven and hell to be in his arms.

Driven by a force stronger than any she had ever known she reached out and unbuttoned Adam's shirt, pulling at it with a kind of mindless frustration, suddenly wanting nothing more than to feel his bare skin against her own. As the shirt parted, she tugged at his shoulders until he was pressed down along the length of her, his muscled chest crushing her breasts, knocking the last bit of air from her lungs.

"God, honey, I'm only human," Adam moaned into her mouth, his self-control stretched to its limit. "I want like hell to make love to you," he confessed, his breath coming hard and fast, "but this isn't the time or the place."

Make love to her? At his words Taylor felt an odd little chill run down her spine. How could he make *love* to her when they barely knew each other? This wasn't love, but physical passion pure and simple. Not that there was anything either pure or simple about it. How could she have been so foolish as to allow the intimacy between them to progress to this point? After all, she wasn't a child. She must have known where this would all lead if nothing was done to stop it. Somewhere, somehow, things had gotten out of hand. And to think that it had been Adam who had called a halt to their lovemaking. . . .

Taylor suddenly realized, much to her mortification, that she was lying half nude beneath him. She wiggled uncomfortably under his weight, wanting nothing more than to end this moment, this night, before she made an even bigger fool of herself than she already had.

As if he sensed her change of heart, Adam gently eased his body from hers and sat up. He raked a hand through his hair, his face dark with some emotion she was loath to name. He sat on the edge of the leather sofa, obviously trying to regain some semblance of control while she struggled to sit up at the other end, her hands visibly shaking as she tugged at her clothing.

The silence between them stretched into one minute and then two before Adam turned and gently place his hand over hers. "I want you, Taylor. I guess that's pretty obvious by now. But I think too much of you, of myself, to make it a one-night stand between us."

She knew he was watching her, but she lacked sufficient courage to meet his eyes. "Adam, I . . ." she stammered to a halt, self-consciously undoing her hand from his.

"Please, let me finish," he said in a soft, insistent voice. "You're a very special woman, Taylor," he added after a brief pause. "You're different from any woman I've ever known. And if and when we do make love, I want it to be something special between us, something we both want without any reservations. Damn, but I selfishly want it to be as perfect as it can be for a man and a woman." Adam brushed his hands across his eyes in a weary gesture. "It's been a long night for both of us. We're tired and we've had one glass of wine too many on top of everything else. I wouldn't want you to ever think I took advantage of the situation."

"You may have noticed I wasn't exactly putting up a fight," she muttered with self-reproach.

"There's nothing for you to be ashamed of, for either of us to be ashamed of. Good Lord, Taylor, we're only human and sometimes human beings do get carried away with their emotions." She sensed that he was speaking with a patience he was far from feeling.

"Perhaps," she replied in an infuriated whisper, her anger directed more at herself than at Adam, "but I'm not the kind of woman who makes a habit of practically falling into bed with a man on the first date."

"And I'm not the kind of man who tries to get every woman he dates into bed with him," he countered indignantly as if to set the record straight. "Let's face it, tonight was something that just—happened."

"Well, it won't happen again," Taylor vowed, her voice shaking with emotion.

"It won't unless you want it to," Adam said noncommittally. Something in his tone made Taylor glance at him, but his expression told her nothing. "C'mon, it's after one. I think I'd better take you home," he suggested with a notable lack of enthusiasm.

She tentatively stood up, wondering if her legs would even support her. "Aren't you forgetting something?"

He gave it about thirty seconds of thought before answering. "Forgetting something? I don't think so."

"I drove tonight. Remember?"

The look on Adam's face was like a dash of icy water. "I still intend to see you home," he said in a voice that clearly meant he would brook no arguments from her.

"Then how will you get home again?" Taylor asked irritably. Didn't he realize that all she wanted was to be left alone?

A determined look crept over Adam's features. "I'll

walk. I've got two perfectly good legs. Believe me, a nice, long walk is just what I need about now."

"You know, it really isn't necessary for you to see me home," Taylor retorted rather crossly.

"I think it is," he said with soft menace, standing to tuck his shirt in the waistband of his trousers. It seemed wise not to argue with him in his present mood.

Taylor glared at the back of his head. "I'll get my purse," she mumbled, not very subtly masking her annoyance. Under other circumstances, she would have preferred a few minutes with a brush and comb. She knew even without looking in a mirror that every speck of lipstick had been kissed from her mouth, that her hair was tousled and in tangles. But all she wanted now was to end this night without any further incident.

With a silent, scowling Adam at her side she walked out to her car. Taylor was almost relieved when he held out his hand and asked for the keys. She wasn't at all certain she trusted herself to drive—not just yet, anyway.

It was a long drive back to Kenton Place that night, with few words exchanged between them, as though each were deep in his own thoughts. Adam drove up to the gates and pressed the button to open them and then pulled into the parking space in front of number 24.

Taylor would have been perfectly willing to say good night to him then and there, but it was apparent that Adam had other plans. He helped her unload her carrying case and clothes from the back of the station wagon. Then she unlocked the front door of the townhouse and turned to face him.

"Thank you for helping me with my things," she

murmured, as he set the cello down inside the door without looking around.

"Any time," he said, straightening back up. A funny little expression flitted across his face. "Damn, we forgot to have our cheesecake!" he swore, snapping his fingers together.

"Yes, we did forget, didn't we?" Taylor agreed, not the least bit interested at that point.

A hint of amusement tugged at the corners of Adam's mouth. Apparently, he was never without his sense of humor for long. "Of course, we did have other things on our minds."

The color rose sharply in Taylor's face. *That* was the understatement of the year, but how boorish of him to remind her of it. And was he laughing at her besides?

"Why don't you go ahead and eat the cheesecake!" she proposed with acid sweetness, secretly hoping he'd choke on it. "Oh, and thank you for inviting me to dinner," she politely added, wishing to avoid any further discussion of the evening's events.

"It was all my pleasure," Adam drawled, reaching out to brush his fingers across her mouth. He bent over and touched his lips to hers in a mere whisper of a kiss. "I'll give you a call tomorrow, honey." Then he turned on his heels and strode off into the night without so much as a glance backwards.

Taylor rather forcefully closed the door after him. "Call all you want, Adam McCord, but you and I are definitely *finis!*" She snapped the chain lock into place. "And what's more, I hate being called *honey!*" She clicked off the hall light and stomped up the stairs to her bedroom.

Forgetting her usual tidy habits, she threw the black dress and high heels in a heap on the nearest chair and began to quickly undress, letting her clothes fall where they might. Taking a nightgown from the bureau drawer, she slipped it on over her head and yanked back the bedcovers. She didn't even bother with her normal routine—her teeth could darn well survive one night without a brushing! With a click of the bedside lamp, Taylor lay there in the darkened room, staring up at the ceiling, her breasts heaving with frustration.

Damn! Damn! Damn! What was it about Adam McCord that turned her into a churning mass of emotions? One minute he had her laughing, the next seething with anger—or trembling with desire, she admitted to herself with brutal honesty. There was something about Adam that brought out all the primitive instincts of her sex. She liked to think that she was a woman of refinement, of discriminating tastes, but he had opened up a Pandora's box and passion, desire, anger—all the baser human emotions she had spent a lifetime condemning—had come tumbling out.

She'd always believed that a human being's life ought to be characterized by finer things—the search for beauty and truth, the striving for perfection, the ability to reason instead of merely to feel. It was often said that art imitates life. Perhaps as an artist she had only been living an imitation as well. It was neither a comforting nor a comfortable thought.

She remembered all too well Adam's kiss, his touch, the frantic racing of her heart under his hand. Perhaps what he aroused in her were not the baser emotions, but something fundamentally human. Apparently, she aroused something equally fundamental and human in him, Taylor thought to herself with a wry smile.

Yet even while she acknowledged the strange attraction between them, she reminded herself that it just didn't make sense. They had so little in common. What was it about one particular man that could set a woman's blood afire while all the others left her cold? And why *this* man of all men? She didn't want to feel this way about Adam, but the choice no longer seemed to be hers. She supposed that passion rarely did make sense.

She had to confess she had never felt more truly alive, more truly a woman, than she did while in Adam's arms. The facts must be faced, not as she wished them to be, but as they were. There was no denying it—she reacted to him as she had to no other man.

"Oh, dear God, what have I gotten myself into?" she cried, uttering a dry sob. Things were no longer clearly black and white, but a sort of muddled gray. Everything had suddenly become so complicated. Talk about a disruptive influence—Adam McCord took the cake!

Of course, she could simply refuse to see him again and that would solve the problem. But that was a coward's way of dealing with life, and Taylor didn't like to think that on top of everything else she was a coward. There came a time for everyone when the choice had to be made—to either reach out and embrace life or turn and run from it. It seemed that her time was here and now.

Taylor nearly jumped out of her skin when the telephone beside her bed rang, its discordant note breaking into the otherwise silent night. As she reached for the receiver in the dark, it was knocked to the bedside table with a resounding thud.

"H-Hello . . ."

"Were you asleep?"

"No, I wasn't asleep," she replied, pushing herself up on the pillow into a sitting position. And she was certainly wide awake now. "Adam, where are you?"

"In a phone booth." He wasn't being overly communicative.

"A phone booth? *Where* in a phone booth?"

Taylor detected what sounded like a weary sigh and her heart went out to him. "I think about a mile from your place."

"You—you sound kind of funny, Adam. Is there anything wrong?"

"Oh, hell! I'm sorry, Taylor. I shouldn't have called you." She could hear the self-disgust in his voice.

"Adam McCord, don't you dare hang up!" she cried into the telephone. Then she lowered her voice again. "Please—don't hang up. I want you to tell me what's wrong." Some time passed and still he didn't answer. It was like pulling teeth. "Adam?"

"You're mad at me, aren't you?" he blurted out.

Taylor started to laugh, then realized he was perfectly serious. "I don't believe this. You're calling at one-thirty in the morning to ask me if I'm mad at you?"

"I guess it sounds pretty stupid when you put it like that," he growled, suddenly rough and surly.

"No—" she corrected him in a gentle voice, twisting the telephone cord around her fingers, "it's not stupid. Actually, I think it's rather sweet."

It was another minute before he responded. "Then you're not mad at me?" he murmured, his mouth close to the receiver.

"Oh, Adam, if it were only that simple," she

groaned. How could she possibly explain to him what she didn't understand herself?

"Will you go out with me again?" He seemed to be holding his breath. "I've *got* to see you again, honey," he breathed huskily.

"All right," she sighed, capitulating, "but it has to be someplace public. Not your apartment and not mine." Taylor knew he would understand the reasons behind her stipulation. She didn't trust either Adam or herself when they were alone.

He didn't seem overly pleased with the idea, but he went along with her, at least for the present. "There's an old movie special playing at one of the local theaters this weekend," he said at last. "Why don't we go on Saturday afternoon?"

What could be the harm in that? It was a public place and in broad daylight to boot. "Okay, I'd like that. What movie is playing, by the way?" she inquired, trying to put their conversation on a less personal footing.

"That, my dear Taylor, is going to be a surprise." Adam softly chuckled. "I'll pick you up at your place around one o'clock on Saturday. And dress casually. I swear some of these old theaters haven't been cleaned in fifty years."

"Adam!" She wrinkled her nose in distaste.

"I was only teasing, honey, but I do recommend you wear jeans or something," he said, still laughing.

"I don't own any jeans," she said, breathing the word like a curse.

"You're kidding!" he scoffed in disbelief.

"No, I'm not kidding," she replied stiffly. Why did she always suspect him of laughing at her?

"Then it's definitely time you bought yourself some,

Miss Jameson. In fact, it wouldn't be a bad idea to buy a couple of pairs. You never know when you're going to need them."

"I suppose so," she grumbled, sounding less than convinced. "I should have time to go shopping tomorrow afternoon."

"I wish I could see you tomorrow," Adam said, suddenly quite serious again. "But I have to work the evening shift."

"Then I'll see you on Saturday," Taylor said lightly, telling herself that, after all, two days wasn't such a very long time.

"Yes, I'll see you on Saturday," he echoed reassuringly.

"It's awfully late, Adam. You'd better go home now."

"Yeah, I guess so," he admitted with reluctance. "Sweet dreams, Taylor."

"You, too." She yawned as she hung up the receiver. Then she snuggled down in her bed for what proved to be a surprisingly good night's sleep.

By twelve-thirty Saturday afternoon, Taylor was dressed and ready to go. She took a last look at herself in the mirror, picked up the leather shoulder bag from the chair in her bedroom and went downstairs. With Adam's admonition in mind, she'd bought herself two pairs of jeans the day before. They sported a well-known designer label on the hip pocket, and she had chosen a blue silk blouse and high-heeled, slip-on sandals to complete the outfit. In short, she looked the picture of casual chic.

All the same, she felt the slightest bit silly in the jeans. Despite her slender, size-six figure, they clung to her body like a second skin. The saleswoman had reassured her that a larger size would appear baggy and therefore even more ridiculous, but Taylor's immediate concern had to do with simply sitting down in the darned things!

This particular Saturday morning had been spent as usual in her well-ordered scheme of things. She had awakened at seven on the dot and in the next four hours had seen to her laundry and grocery shopping and cleaning her apartment. It wasn't that Taylor was particularly enamored of housework; she simply recognized that it was unavoidable. Like anyone who led a busy life, she had a schedule and she stuck to it rigidly. She would be the first to admit that flexibility wasn't one of her virtues.

She'd just finished making a pitcher of fresh iced tea when the doorbell rang. She quickly dried her hands and put the pitcher in the refrigerator before going to answer it.

Adam was casually leaning against the porch wall gazing off into the distance. In those few seconds before he turned to her, Taylor made a quick study of his lean form in the jeans and shirt he was wearing. She nearly let out a wolf whistle in imitation of Rocky's several nights before. Adam was a picture of virility in jeans that snugly encased his hips and thighs. His short-sleeved shirt did little to hide his well-developed arms and chest. Taylor had to admit he had never looked better. Her heart picked up speed; her palms were suddenly damp. Her iron resolve seemed a fragile thing indeed in the face of his compelling presence.

Adam turned and looked down at her, his face breaking into an appreciative smile. "I've always wondered what tight jeans would look like on a truly classy woman," he murmured, unabashedly looking her over from head to toe. "This sure beats anything I ever imagined."

Taylor felt a telltale blush rise to her cheeks. "I told the saleswoman they were too tight, but she kept insisting this was the only way to wear the darned things."

"In your case, she was absolutely right." Adam grinned in a way that did little to dispel her embarrassment.

"I hope you realize I'll have to stand through the whole movie," she hastened to explain. "I can't sit down in these things and still breathe."

"It'll get better once you break them in," Adam informed her, obviously speaking with a voice of authority on the subject of jeans. His own looked like they'd been through at least two wars and barely survived.

"And how long does that take?" she shot back.

He thoughtfully rubbed a hand across his chin. "If you wear them a lot—maybe a year or so."

"A year or so! You mean to tell me I have to suffer through a whole year this way?"

"We all have at one time or another." He shrugged. "I'm afraid it's the price we each have to pay. . . ."

"Well, I have no intention of paying *that* particular price, thanks anyway," she retorted, turning around to head back inside. "Come on in while I get my handbag," she said over her shoulder.

She heard Adam close the front door behind him as she went along to the living room where she'd left her bag and a light sweater on the chair.

"This is nice . . . *very* nice," she heard him exclaim.

"That's right—you haven't been here before, have you?" she responded evenly.

He wasn't the least bit fooled by her nonchalance. "I think you know well enough that I haven't," he drawled. "Did you decorate it yourself?" he went on to inquire with genuine interest as he looked around.

"Yes, I did," she said, warming to the subject. "It's been kind of a hobby of mine."

Adam continued with no trace of sarcasm in his voice. "You obviously have excellent taste in everything." He turned, his gaze leveled at her. "My apartment must have come as quite a shock to you."

"Not at all," she declared, meeting his gaze. "It has a lived-in look to it. Actually, it's very much like you."

"I'm not sure that's a compliment to either me or the apartment," he retorted only half humorously. "Are you ready to go?"

"Yes, I am." Taylor nodded, slipping the handbag over one arm and the sweater over the other.

It soon became apparent that the theater he was taking her to was halfway across town. Traffic on a busy Saturday afternoon in Knoxville made the drive quite lengthy. Adam found a parking lot a block from the old movie house and pulled into one of the few remaining spaces. He reached around behind him to take something from the back seat before getting out of the gray sedan and coming around to open her door.

Taylor looked down at his hand with curiosity. "What's in the sack?"

"Caramel corn," he told her with a perfectly straight

face. She held back the smart retort on the tip of her tongue just in the nick of time. "It doesn't seem like a movie to me without caramel corn and they never sell it at places like this," Adam explained, then regarded her for a moment with more than a hint of suspicion in his dark eyes. "Why? Do you mind?"

"Heavens, no," she laughed. "As a matter of fact, I love caramel corn."

Her reward for giving him the correct answer was a dazzling smile. "And here I bet you've been asking yourself what we could possibly have in common," he remarked with an unerring accuracy for hitting the mark.

"A relationship is based on more than a bag of caramel corn," she pontificated, then burst out laughing at the utter ridiculousness of her own statement.

Adam stopped in the middle of the sidewalk and looked down at her with an incredulous expression on his face. "Do you realize that's the first time I've heard you laugh at *yourself?*"

"Normally, *you* seem to find me amusing enough for the both of us," Taylor pointed out, rather pleased with the way she tossed that off.

A healthy, robust laugh shook Adam's chest. "Touché, honey—again!" He brought himself under control as he stepped up to the window to buy their tickets.

"Adam—" There was an odd little hitch in Taylor's voice that immediately drew his attention.

"What is it, honey?" he asked, suddenly all concern.

"Are you going to tell me that we drove all the way out here to see *this?*" she demanded, gazing up at the marquee. She proceeded to read aloud from the two-foot letters emblazoned above their heads. "Twelve exciting chapters of *The Adventures of Captain Marvel?*"

The sheepish grin on Adam's face was her answer. He bit his lip, looking about twelve years old. "Trust me?"

5

〜〜〜〜〜〜〜〜〜〜〜

And just how *long* will it take to watch twelve episodes of Captain Marvel's adventures?" Taylor demanded, tapping her foot impatiently.

Adam cleared his throat several times. "Three hours, more or less," he mumbled into his shirt collar. Taking her firmly by the elbow, he whisked Taylor through the theater door, thrusting their tickets into the usher's hand as they went by. "Trust me, you're going to love this!"

They stopped to buy soft drinks at the refreshment stand before finding their way into the dimly lit theater. Taylor was surprised to see that the greatest percentage of the audience appeared to be adults over the age of thirty. Apparently, Adam was not the only one choosing to relive his childhood on this particular Saturday afternoon.

"So, tell me," she said, once they were settled in their seats, "exactly who is Captain Marvel?"

"Are you sure you want to know that? I wouldn't want to ruin the movie for you," Adam said solicitously.

"I don't think that's possible," she murmured in a dry tone.

"Well, you see," Adam leaned toward her, lowering his voice conspiratorially, "Captain Marvel is really young Billy Batson. Or I should say that Billy Batson turns into Captain Marvel when he repeats the name of the old man who appears to him in the tomb of the Scorpion."

"The Scorpion?"

"Yeah, that's the bad guy," he told her in all seriousness.

"Then I assume that the old man is a good guy," Taylor ventured, trying her best to get into the spirit of the occasion. She'd never been very childlike even as a child.

Adam nodded. "The old man is Shazam himself."

"Shazam?" Her voice broke on the word.

"Yes, Shazam. You know, the wisdom of Solomon, the strength of Hercules, the stamina of Atlas, the power of Zeus, the courage of Achilles and the speed of Mercury," he recited as if he were reading from an old comic book.

"You've seen this before, haven't you?" Taylor said accusingly.

"When I was a kid back in our old neighborhood in Pittsburgh," he admitted. "The serials were actually before my time, but the manager of the local theater was something of an old-movie buff. Every Saturday afternoon he'd show one chapter of a classic serial before the main attraction. *The Adventures of Captain Marvel* is considered one of the finest serials ever made. Wait until you see the flying sequences. They're amazing when you remember this was filmed in 1941."

"I have a feeling this whole afternoon is going to be pretty amazing," she quipped, digging her fingers into the paper sack for a handful of caramel-covered popcorn.

Adam slid down in his seat as the credits began to roll on the big screen in front of them. "I'll bet you've never seen anything like this before in your life," he said softly, as if there were a rare treat in store for her.

"A sure bet if I ever heard one," Taylor muttered under her breath.

What she hadn't realized was that audience participation was frequently part of a Saturday afternoon like this one. The first time it happened she was dumbstruck. The second time she found herself laughing out loud at the others in the theater, including Adam. By the end of the fifth episode, she let herself go and wholeheartedly joined in the fun.

Every time Billy Batson recited the old man's name and in a puff of smoke miraculously became none other than Captain Marvel, every voice in the theater called out "Shazam" along with him. It was crazy, but Taylor realized she had never enjoyed herself more.

During the brief intermission they wandered into the lobby where she excused herself to wash her sticky fingers. Adam was patiently waiting for her when she came out of the ladies' room, reminding her of another time when he had been there waiting for her.

He could easily become a habit with her, Taylor admitted to herself. And a bad habit at that.

"Let's get back before the bombs are dropped on the shack where Billy and Betty are being held captive," Adam urged, slipping a proprietary arm about her shoulders. He was referring to the latest predicament their hero had managed to get himself into.

Adam's arm remained around her even after they'd returned to their seats, proving to be a far greater distraction to Taylor than any action on the screen. She basked in his warmth, inhaling the scent she was beginning to identify as distinctly his. She reached up and placed her hand on the one he casually rested on her shoulder, feeling the understated strength in the fingers that interlocked with hers, noting the way her hand nestled perfectly within his larger one.

There was sensitivity as well as strength in those hands. She could attest to that. She remembered all too vividly the need incited by their touch, the wild desires created by their caress. And she had thought herself clever by insisting on a public place! There was no haven, no place of safety, as long as she carried with her the memory of him and the passion he could arouse in her.

Without warning tears welled up in Taylor's eyes. It would be so easy to fall in love with him. She quickly turned her head away. She couldn't be falling in love with him. She absolutely refused to! They were as different as night and day. Yet Adam affected her in ways she'd never dreamt possible. Was this the way love came? Like a thief in the night? Did it always sneak up on some poor, unsuspecting fool like herself who presumed she was immune to love unlike the rest of the human race?

Adam had once told her that she was different from any woman he'd ever known. Well, she could say the same of him. He was different from any man she had ever known. She was woman enough to recognize that he wanted her, but that did not necessarily mean that love entered into the picture. And even if love did enter in, was it enough to bridge the awful gap between them? Could love ever be strong enough to create a world of its own between two people from such totally different spheres?

For the first time in her twenty-seven years, Taylor found that reason was no help at all. Logical thinking had its place, but it was of little use when it came to something as volatile as emotions. To think that she claimed to be a teacher when she had so much to learn herself! How dare she tell her students how to inject emotion into their music when she so proudly claimed to be devoid of emotion herself?

But was she? Or did it only take the right man to unlock any woman's heart? In some way she couldn't begin to explain, she hungered for this man, for his touch, for his kiss. She wanted Adam as she'd never wanted a man before. She wanted him in a hundred ways. And if he wanted her as well, then how could she resist satisfying his hunger as well as her own?

Taylor slowly turned her head to look at him, intently studying him as if by doing so she would somehow find the answers to all her questions. Adam must have sensed that her attention wasn't on the movie for he turned toward her, his eyes clearly visible in the darkness.

"My God, Taylor, don't look at me like that!" he growled in a hoarse whisper, drawing her closer.

"Don't look at you like *what?*" she asked in a small voice, her mouth almost touching his. She had no way of knowing that for a moment the hunger she felt had been plainly written on her face for him to see.

"Let's get the hell out of here!" he swore, his lips tightening into a thin, tense line.

"No—let's stay to see the end," she softly argued, her courage faltering at the last minute. With a supreme effort of will, she dragged her gaze from his and stared up at the screen with unseeing eyes.

The rest of the movie was a form of exquisite torture. Adam scarcely took his eyes from her. Taylor was aware of his fingers caressing her neck, the tip of her ear, the skin beneath her collar. His thigh was pressed against her leg, a less than subtle reminder of the physical attraction that had grown into a tangible force between them. She had no one to blame but herself. She had started something without the courage to see it through to the end.

When the last frame froze on the screen the houselights came up and the theater began to quickly empty. Adam sat there, making no move to rise from his seat.

"We've got to talk," he said, bringing her closer to the assertive length of his lean body.

Taylor wasn't at all convinced that talking was what he had in mind. "I really don't think this is the time or place, Adam," she pointed out in the identical words he'd once used with her.

"Dammit, it's never the right time or place!" he grated impatiently, jumping to his feet. He grasped her by the hand and pulled her up alongside him. "You're driving me out of my mind. I hope you realize that," he said in an exasperated tone.

She felt a tingle of pleasure at his admission. Then at once berated herself for it. She was going out of her mind, too, and there wasn't anything pleasurable about it.

They were halfway up the aisle when she hesitated, tugging at his hand. "Adam—wait! I forgot my sweater."

"I'll get it," he rasped, leaving her there while he retraced his steps to their seats. He walked back toward her with determined strides, draping the sweater about her shoulders. "I'd forgotten this anyway," he commented, dumping the paper sack in a trash barrel as they walked into the lobby.

Neither spoke on the way to his car, finding that words did not come so easily after all. Once inside the gray sedan, Adam reached into the back seat and turned to hand her the Dashiell Hammett book she'd meant to take home with her.

"I wasn't sure if you'd forgotten this the other night or if you simply weren't that interested in reading it," he said with a deceptive nonchalance which somehow made her all the more aware of the tension behind his words.

"I-I am interested in reading it," she stammered, strangely touched by the thoughtful gesture. "Thank you for bringing it, Adam." She clutched the book to her, a sharp corner digging into her breast through the flimsy protection of the silk shirt, reminding her of the almost painful pleasure afforded by his touch.

"You're welcome," he mumbled with an impersonal politeness that hurt more than it should have.

It hurt, too, to realize that she was the cause of the deep, scowling lines of frustration on his face. But then what did she expect? Taylor demanded of herself as Adam maneuvered the car out of the parking lot and into the flow of traffic. Talk about blowing hot and cold! If only things between them weren't moving so fast. There had been no time to get to know each other as friends, no time to gain each other's trust and confidence. There had been no time to talk of mundane matters and now each was afraid to be the first to speak.

She caught herself daydreaming, not realizing where Adam was taking her until she looked up and saw the entrance to the park. Late-afternoon shadows were playing hide and seek in the lush, green surroundings. It was quiet and peaceful, with just a hint of autumn in the air. Adam pulled up in a secluded corner and killed the engine, sitting there staring straight ahead of him.

"You . . ." Taylor swallowed and tried again. "You did say we had to talk," she prompted, fighting back the feeling of suffocation that gripped her throat.

He hesitated a moment. "Let's walk," he finally suggested, opening the car door.

Taylor eagerly got out and met him halfway, finding relief in simply standing in the too-tight jeans instead of sitting. In unspoken accord they fell into step, sauntering down the nearest path, which cut through a heavily wooded area and up a small hillside.

She'd never been the outdoor type, but it felt good to be in the fresh air. Perhaps this was what she had needed all along to clear the cobwebs from her brain. Problems always seemed less looming when put in the perspective of something larger than one's self, like the tall poplars and pines that crowded both sides of the narrow path.

They must have walked for ten minutes or more without speaking a word. Taylor was hesitant to break the silence between them, aware of the tension gradually easing in the tall form of the man beside her. He was the outdoor type—that was plain to see. Unmindful of the wind that tousled his hair, Adam seemed to be in his natural element. He was taking in huge gulps of the fresh air as if the close confines of the theater and the car had been suffocating to him.

"I love it out here!" he finally burst out as though the words could no longer be contained, his pace picking up speed as if he found some measure of relief in the sheer exercise of his long, muscular legs. "I've always spent as much time as I could out-of-doors," he added, without the slightest sign of becoming winded. Taylor was finding it a challenge just to keep pace with the stride he set for them both. "Sorry about that," Adam apologized, suddenly realizing that she was having difficulty in keeping up with him. "I'd forgotten what short legs you have."

"I don't have short legs," Taylor shot back. "It's the shoes." She'd always been a little more than self-conscious about her height. She didn't need any snide remarks from an overgrown "nature lover."

"I can see they weren't made with hiking in mind," he said with a perfectly straight face as she nearly teetered off the three-inch heels. "Do you like to go camping?" he asked, continuing their walk at a more reasonable speed.

"Camping?" He was joking, of course.

"Yes, you know, camping—with sleeping bags and

a tent. Sitting around an open campfire, gazing up at the stars overhead."

"That's what I thought you meant." She grimaced, thinking of the creatures no doubt underfoot while he had his head in the stars.

"Hey, I've got a great idea, honey!" Adam stopped dead in his tracks, grabbing her by the arm.

Another one? she nearly muttered under her breath. "What's that?" she asked aloud, not sure she wanted to hear this latest "great idea" of his.

"Why don't we go camping in the Smoky Mountains next weekend?" He obviously thought this idea was on a par with Columbus discovering America and Edison inventing the lightbulb.

"I—ah—really don't think I'm cut out for camping," she said evasively, studying the tip of her sandals in intimate detail.

"Have you ever been camping?" Adam demanded to know in a lion's roar of a voice.

"Not all of us feel a need to get *that* close to nature, Adam McCord," she said in her own defense.

"Didn't your parents ever take you camping when you were a kid?" The accusation in his tone was unmistakable.

"My parents' idea of camping out was to stay at a hotel with a less than five-star restaurant," she informed him haughtily.

He looked at her as if she were a poor, deprived child. "Well, better late than never," he said briskly, taking it for granted she would agree to go with him.

"Besides," she reasoned, stalling for time, "I don't have a sleeping bag or any of the equipment you need to go camping."

"No problem, I have enough for both of us," he assured her. Somehow she had known he was going to say that. "I don't have to work next weekend. We could leave Friday about noon and drive down through Pigeon Forge and Gatlinburg and into the Smokies from there."

"Adam—" Was he always like a steamroller once he got started? "I really don't like camping out."

"But you've never tried it," he pointed out, puzzled by her attitude. "How do you know you don't like it?"

"Trust me," she said dryly.

"Will you promise to at least think about it?" It was a genuine request, not a demand.

"All right, I'll think about it, but that's all I promise to do," she replied honestly. Apparently, that satisfied him for the time being. At least, he didn't badger her on the subject as they resumed their walk. It was some fifteen minutes and countless little stones in her shoes later that Taylor knew her feet deserved a rest even if she didn't. "Would you mind if we stopped for a few minutes? These shoes really weren't meant for walking on a dirt path like this."

"Have the good sense to leave those things at home when we go camping," Adam remarked without thinking. At the exasperated look on her face, he threw his hands up in an expressive shrug. "Sorry—I shouldn't have mentioned it. It won't happen again." He led her off the path and into a small clearing. "It's too damp to sit on the ground," he noted, drawing her toward him. "So I'll just lean against the tree and you can lean against me." His arms went around her waist in demonstration.

It wasn't at all what Taylor had had in mind when she suggested taking a break, but some part of her wanted to be closer to him even while her common sense told her to back off. She placed her hands lightly on his chest, intending to use them for leverage if absolutely necessary.

"Is that better?" Adam murmured, his lion's roar no more than a purr now.

"No—I mean, yes," she said, turning crimson and stumbling over the words. "It's getting chilly," she went on with forced calmness. "I wish I'd brought my sweater with me."

"Oh, honey, that's an invitation if I ever heard one," Adam taunted gently. "I can guarantee you won't need a sweater to keep you warm." He wrapped his arms tightly around her, bringing her up against the full length of his body.

She was an idiot! An absolute idiot! Every time she was with him she opened her mouth and put her foot in it. Her whole foot! Yet she felt the heat of his body slowly seep through to her own, indeed warming her as no sweater could ever have done. And when he bent to softly nuzzle her neck, she felt rather than heard a great sigh come from his chest.

"Adam, we're in a public park." Her words came out in a whisper.

He didn't bother to look up. "There's no one around here. We haven't seen another living soul since we got out of the car except for the birds and the bees. And I doubt if there's anything we can teach them that they don't already know." Then he kissed her long and languorously, not caring who saw them.

It was a kiss that made her forget where she was or even who she was. She was only aware of Adam— Adam and the madness he could create in her with his lips and his tongue and his teeth. She'd never been so thoroughly or so beautifully kissed by anyone in her entire life. His kiss told her she was desirable, irresistible, as essential to him as the air he breathed. He asked for her response instead of demanding it, and so she gave it of her own free will.

And there in her kiss, in the touch of her hands as they anchored themselves in the fine hair at his nape, was the hunger she had tried so hard to conceal from herself as well as from him. There was no sense in denying it. God help her, but she wanted this man and there was no mistaking the fact that he wanted her as well.

It was there in the way he lingered over the sweetness of her mouth, in the way his hands moved up and down her body to finally settle in the small of her back, pressing her to him, making her unashamedly aware of the physical form that his need took. The hard reality of that male need pressed against her thigh, and she knew this was no longer some kind of game between them, but truly the passion of a man and a woman.

Adam gradually spread his legs apart, settling her between them, rubbing his body against hers with a mindless desire that shook them both to the core. Taylor felt an irresistible urge to touch him, to feel him shudder in her arms, to have his need for her override any semblance of rational thought he might still possess.

She leaned into him, her hands clutching at the belt about his waist. She ran the tip of her tongue along his lip, nipping at the vulnerable flesh at the corners of his mouth until his lips came down on hers, hard and hungry. She felt his control begin to slip and urged him on, knowing that wherever his desire took him she would also go.

She foolishly thought herself in control, but how quickly, how easily, how irrefutably, she was proven wrong. His hands slipped up her back and around to span her rib cage, his thumbs extended to tease the hardening nipple of each breast. She heard a low moan of desire rise from her throat only to be swallowed up by the mouth fused to hers. She felt her body beg for his caress, her flesh plead for that ultimate union with his.

Concealed by the shadows of approaching night, Adam pulled the blouse free of her jeans, one hand surreptitiously slipping beneath to find her warmth. He ran his palm across the smooth skin of her abdomen and then up to cup the underside of one breast, discovering there a small mole. He studied its tiny form before moving on to the ivory mound with its expectant peak waiting for his possession. His fingers insinuated themselves under the lacy barrier to their final destination. As he found her with the tantalizing tip of his nail, she was unable to withhold his name from her lips.

"Adam! Touch me! Please touch me!" she cried out in little gasps against his mouth.

He crushed her gently within the velvet strength of his grip. "Touch you? Dear God, I want to bury myself in your sweet body," he rasped, as if it were pure torture not to be able to do so. His other hand circled her waist just inside her jeans, fingering the satiny layer that separated her from him. "I need your touch, honey. I need to feel your hands on me," he pleaded persuasively.

And she suddenly found that she needed to touch him, to excite him to the same feverish pitch to which he had driven her, to take him to the edge of the madness that firmly held her in its grasp. Taylor reached out and lightly ran her hands over the prominent bone and muscle of his chest, and down to his taut waistline. She couldn't seem to get enough of him. He was the most wondrous thing she had ever held in her hands. Her fingers shyly skirted his thigh, then boldly reached behind him to outline the curve of his sinewy leg. As she trailed her hands around to the front of his body, she felt him tremble within her feminine embrace.

"Taylor!" Her name was agony and ecstasy on his lips. She was both his heaven and his own private hell. She was everything he had dreamt she could be and so much more. She was more woman in that slight, slender body of hers than even he had imagined.

With a terrifying need he fitted her to him, his mouth clamping down on hers as if it would take an earth-shattering catastrophe to drive them apart. In the end it was nothing more than the lights of an approaching car that brought them to their senses, that made them aware of their surroundings and the lack of privacy the park afforded.

Adam gently held her within his embrace as they both fought for the control they had surrendered in each other's arms. It was some minutes before either was capable of speaking.

Groping to recover his inner balance, he grated, "Damn, honey, you make me lose my head! In a couple of minutes I think I would have made love to you right here and now and said to hell with the consequences!"

Taylor stood there staring at him, suddenly aware that she could survive a loss of dignity with this man and not feel ashamed afterwards. Indeed, she just had. It was a startling revelation for a woman whose whole life had been based on the principle of dignity and discipline first. Somehow with Adam all her noble ideals were no more than ashes in the wind. But then what were noble ideals in the face of the mindless passion he could arouse in her?

"Oh, Adam, somehow I don't seem like myself when I'm with you," she confessed, resting her head on his chest, listening to the rapid beating of his heart beneath her cheek and knowing that its cadence matched the racing of her own heart.

"And I suppose you think I'm the cool, levelheaded police detective when I'm with you," he mused sarcastically. "Let's face it. We seem to have this strange effect on each other. We're a couple of Dr. Jekylls and Mr. Hydes when we get around one another."

"What are we going to do about it?" Taylor ventured in a small voice, burying her face even deeper in his shirt.

"I don't know, honey." He shook his head in bewilderment. "All I do know is that we're like a walking time bomb and that sooner or later all hell is going to break loose," he growled in a soft, gruff voice. "It's starting to get dark. We'd better head back to the car while we can still see our way."

Taylor tried to tuck her shirt back into the waistband of her jeans, making a thoroughly inadequate job of it. The pants were too snug without undoing the zipper, and she had no intention of doing that in front of Adam. She finally gave up and signaled that she was ready to start back.

A kind of thoughtful silence descended between them as they walked, broken only by an occasional idle comment from one or the other. The walk seemed to take twice as long as it had initially. Taylor felt a genuine sense of relief when the gray sedan came into view.

She pushed the sweater and book out of the way as she got into the front passenger seat, watching with huge gray eyes as Adam strode around to the door on the other side. He eased his long legs behind the wheel and then sat there, once again silently staring straight ahead of him.

"I've always believed that honesty is really the best policy, Taylor," he began, finding that the words did not come easily. He took a deep breath and plunged on, his knuckles white with tension as he gripped the steering wheel in front of him. "I want you as I've never wanted anything or anyone in my life. I-I can't explain it. I only know it's the truth." Then he caught his breath; it sounded like a groan. "Sweet Jesus, it's tearing my guts apart!"

"Oh, Adam—" She reached out and placed her hand on his arm, feeling the tiny quiver her touch created in his taut muscles.

He turned the full force of his burning gaze on her, and his words spewed forth with the vengeance of an erupting volcano. "Once we make love—and we will sooner or later, make no mistake about that—there will be no going back for either one of us. It will be a commitment we'll have to live with for a long time to come. I want you to be very sure before that happens." His voice grew softer, if no less intense. "Once you're mine, once I'm yours, neither of us will ever be truly free again. If you're honest with yourself, then you know that as surely as I do."

"Adam, you're frightening me," she whispered, the breath shuddering in her lungs.

"Then that makes us even because you scare the hell out of me, lady!" he exclaimed. "We're not a couple of naive kids rushing into this in the heat of passion. As mature adults, we owe it to ourselves to go into this with our eyes wide open. Because whatever comes will ultimately be our responsibility and no one else's."

Taylor reluctantly nodded her head. "Yes, I know," she admitted.

"I can't take a physical relationship with you casually. I'm already emotionally involved with you right up to my damned neck. I can't take that last step and go in over my head unless I know for certain that you'll be there for me. I don't want to make any mistakes with you, Taylor. You're too important to me. I guess what I'm trying to say is that I don't want to have *sex* with you."

"You don't?" she rasped, her heart stuck somewhere in the region of her throat.

"No, I don't." He paused significantly. "I want to make *love* to you."

She found she had no words to reply. Damn him! It would be so much easier if he didn't demand that she *feel,* if he would only allow her to *think!* She didn't trust feelings. She never had. And yet that was exactly what Adam was asking her to do. Quickly, what did she feel? She must know. He was sitting there, taut as a bow string, waiting for her to say something, anything.

The color slowly drained from his face, leaving him as pale as death itself. "Apparently, I've made a hell of a mistake." His deep voice was bitingly sarcastic. "I thought you felt the same way I did."

"But I do!" The words were out before she even realized she had opened her mouth.

"Thank God!" he intoned, with a glint of satisfaction in his eye. "Don't look so worried, honey. I'm not asking you to sign an affidavit in your own blood."

"Oh, but you've drawn blood, Adam McCord. Make no mistake about that!" she informed him, laughing unexpectedly and uncomfortably. It was a laugh that bordered on hysteria.

"But I'll always be there to bind up your wounds," he promised in a voice so soft it nearly brought tears to her eyes. "You can trust me, Taylor. You may not believe that now, but you can."

"I hope so," she whispered, pulling herself together with a visible effort, "because once trust is lost between two people there's no way this side of heaven to get it back."

"Then we'll make certain we don't do anything to lose it," Adam vowed, moving to bring her face up to his. He sealed that vow with an exquisitely tender kiss, a kiss that said far more than any words between them ever could. "And just to prove how trustworthy I am," he said almost humorously as he pulled away from her, "I'm going to take you home and leave you on your doorstep with a chaste kiss good night."

"Not too chaste, I hope," she breathed, trembling, trying to return his smile and finding it wasn't totally impossible. How strange that she should feel like laughing. But then wasn't laughter the flipside of tears?

"Oh, woman, what am I going to do about you?" he asked, giving her a little shake.

"I don't know," she murmured, giving it serious consideration. "I have the same problem. What am I going to do about you?" She had to face the possibility that Adam was more than she could handle. No, by God, Taylor thought rebelliously, she was enough of a woman to handle any man! Even this man!

"It's a problem we'll have to work out together," Adam proposed, providing a mild diversion by revving the engine of the sedan and driving out of the park.

The good-night kiss between them wasn't quite as chaste as either had planned. In truth, one thing seemed to lead to another until they were both trembling with reaction when they finally drew apart.

Adam propped himself against the front door of the townhouse for support. "I should have my damned head examined!" he concluded wryly. "I'm actually thinking of walking away from you tonight when all I really want to do is sweep you up in my arms, carry you through that door and barricade it shut behind us."

"Wouldn't a simple request on your part suffice?" Taylor pointed out. Flirting with danger was proving to be a heady intoxicant.

Adam's eyes narrowed perceptibly. "And what if I did ask to spend the night with you?"

It was Taylor's turn to hesitate. "Are you asking?"

"Still playing games, aren't you?" he observed scornfully. "No, I'm not asking, but don't kid yourself, honey. If I did want you tonight I wouldn't have to ask."

"That sure of me, huh?" she plunged in recklessly.

Adam caught the tip of her chin in his hand and forced her to meet his gaze. "No, I'm that sure of myself, and next time I don't intend to *ask*."

"Well, forewarned is forearmed, as they say," Taylor countered flippantly.

"Forearm all you want," he commented dryly. "A good cop always gets his man—or hadn't you heard?" Adam turned and walked down the sidewalk toward his car. "Oh—and I suggest you get yourself a pair of decent walking shoes before next weekend," he tossed over his shoulder.

"And why, pray tell, would I want to do something like that?" Taylor asked him loftily.

Adam paused with his hand on the car door, grinning up at her. "Because you can't wear high heels to go camping, of course." With that parting shot, he got into his car and drove off.

"Camping, my foot!" Taylor was sputtering as she unlocked the front door of her apartment. "Hell would have to freeze over first, Adam McCord. . . ."

6

It was nearly noon. Taylor was gazing out the kitchen window as she sipped the last of her chamomile tea. The sun was high and bright in a vivid blue sky, the day pleasantly warm and breezy for the first week of October. Not the kind of day one would have expected hell to freeze over, she thought to herself with a wry little smile.

But then she supposed almost anything was possible when one was dealing with Adam McCord. She was going camping, wasn't she?

She glanced at the soft-sided bag sitting in the hallway and mentally ran down the list of items she had packed according to Adam's instructions. There were two pairs of jeans, a comfortable size eight this time, two warm pullover sweaters, several pairs of thick cotton socks, an all-purpose windbreaker, a pair

113

of gloves, several changes of underwear, a towel and washcloth, and sundry personal items.

Considering the almost summery weather Knoxville was having, she would have assumed all this warm clothing was unnecessary. But Adam had assured her that in the mountain altitudes temperatures ranged from fifteen to twenty degrees cooler than those in the valley areas. Apparently, the Great Smoky Mountains were known for their clear days and cool nights at this time of the year.

Fastidious to the end, Taylor rinsed out her teacup and set it in the drain rack to one side of the stainless steel sink. The borrowed picnic cooler sitting on the counter was filled to the brim with the food she had insisted on bringing as her fair share for the weekend. Although the subject of money had never been discussed between them, she was quite sure that she had more to spare than Adam. And it wasn't cast in stone anywhere she knew of that only the man could spend his money on dates.

Not that this was exactly her idea of a date. In fact, she still wasn't sure just when or even why she had agreed to go along with this crazy scheme of his. Adam's campaign had been both strategic and subtle from beginning to end. He had assumed that sooner or later she would break down and agree to go.

He had mentioned at every opportunity the breathtaking pageantry of color in the mountains in the autumn, the seemingly endless array of yellows, reds, browns and purples. He had hailed the majestic peaks softened by a forest mantle, stretching away to remote horizons, the smokelike mist that rose from the dense plant life. He had extolled the hundreds of miles of trails that wound along crystal-clear streams and waterfalls, past dense forests to bright vistas that unexpectedly opened on mile after mile of rolling mountain slopes.

He had even thrown in a few references to the two hundred kinds of birds that had been observed in the Great Smokies and the numerous varieties of wildlife from the black bear to the white-tailed deer to the rare, but occasional, bobcat that might appear on or near the road.

Well, perhaps Adam hadn't been so subtle after all, maybe only relentless. In the end, Taylor wasn't sure if she had agreed to go out of curiosity or sheer exhaustion. Whatever the reason, there she stood in jeans and cotton shirt, hiking boots and thick socks that stretched all the way up to her knees. Her hair was pulled back in a long ponytail and secured with a brightly colored bandana. She'd loosely tied a sweater about her shoulders and perched a pair of dark sunglasses atop her head. It was twelve o'clock on the dot and she was ready. As ready as she'd ever be. . . .

As if he'd been standing right outside counting the chimes of the small clock in her front hall, she heard a brisk knock at the door on the stroke of twelve and knew that it was Adam. If nothing else, the man was punctual.

"Coming!" Taylor called out as she went to open the door for him.

Adam was standing there framed in the doorway, looking like some modern-day version of Daniel Boone, with a big grin on his face.

"Hi, honey!" He dropped a quick kiss on the tip of her nose as he charged past her to the overnight bag sitting in the middle of the hall floor. "I see you're packed and ready to go." That seemed to please him immensely.

"You did say noon," she confirmed, amused by his obvious enthusiasm. An enthusiasm that was *almost* contagious. "I can take my bag if you want to get the cooler in the kitchen." There was no sense in making two trips between the townhouse and his car if one would do it.

"I'll get the cooler then," Adam remarked after brief consideration.

Taylor took one last look around and then picked up her bag and followed him out the door, turning the knob behind her to make sure it was securely locked.

"Where in the world did you get that?" she inquired, astonished to see a large, four-wheel drive vehicle parked where she had expected to see his sedan.

"One of my friends in the department loaned it to me for the weekend," Adam told her, stowing the cooler in the rear. "Here, I'll take that," he insisted, holding his hand out for her overnight bag.

"What is all this stuff?" she laughed incredulously, looking inside the four-wheel drive.

"A tent, sleeping bags, air mattresses, propane lantern, a Colman stove in case it rains and we can't cook over a campfire, hatchet, binoculars, drinking water, canteens, cooking utensils, flashlight, shovel . . ."

"All right! Enough!" Taylor interrupted. "I'm almost sorry I asked. Do you always haul all this—this paraphernalia along when you go camping?"

"I tend to travel lighter than this when I go alone,

but for your first time out I thought you would appreciate having all the conveniences of home."

Hardly all the conveniences of home in her opinion, but Taylor refrained from saying so aloud as Adam opened the passenger door and gave her a hand up. "Do you often go camping by yourself?" she asked instead as he settled his long form in the driver's seat.

"Whenever I get the chance." Adam's expression was suddenly one of utter seriousness. "I found out a long time ago, honey, that going off by myself helps to put a lot of things in perspective. It honestly helps me deal with the recurrent cynicism that goes with the job of being a policeman." He dropped the subject and his serious expression as he gazed through the window at the cloudless sky overhead. "It sure looks like we're going to have good weather on our side."

"Hmmph! Good weather or not, I'd like to know how you always manage to talk me into doing things I don't want to," she teased, her tone only half humorous.

Adam put his head back and laughed. "Wait until I try to talk you into something you do want to do!"

With that they started out, heading east from Knoxville toward Sevierville, named for the first governor of Tennessee, and on through Pigeon Forge and Gatlinburg. Gatlinburg was officially known as the host town of the Great Smoky Mountains as well as a center for mountain arts and crafts.

"Boy, Gatlinburg has sure turned into a tourist trap," Adam muttered, shaking his head, as they drove down the main street of the small town. "You have to go out on Highway 73 away from the center of town to see the real craftsmen at work. That's where the potters, weavers, woodcarvers and others have their shops. With the resurgence of traditional crafts under the auspices of the Smoky Mountain Arts and Crafts Community, some of this will be eliminated, I hope."

"I haven't been here recently, but several years ago I drove down with a friend and we rode the 'Ober Gatlinburg' cable car up to Mount Harrison. There were some beautiful ski chalets visible on the mountainside," Taylor added.

"Yes, this has become quite a year-round ski area, too. Do you ski?"

"Good heavens, no!" she exclaimed. "Do you?"

"I've never had a chance to try it, but I'd like to some day," Adam confessed as they left Gatlinburg behind them and entered the national park itself. They stopped at park headquarters where they registered and chose their campsite. "We'll take the loop over to Cades Cove and then on to our site," Adam told her as they walked back to the borrowed Blazer.

"It looks awfully isolated where we're going," Taylor commented, studying the map the park ranger had given them.

"That's the whole idea, honey. Don't worry—I know what I'm doing," Adam chuckled reassuringly.

"I suppose the next thing you're going to try to tell me is that you were once a Boy Scout," she suggested with a sardonic lift of a blond brow.

"As a matter of fact, I made Eagle Scout and Order of the Arrow while I was in high school," he said with a perfectly straight face.

"It figures," Taylor mumbled under her breath. "Well, I wasn't a Girl Scout, Adam McCord, so you're on your own. I don't know the first thing about putting up a tent or rubbing two sticks together."

"In that case, it's a good thing I brought plenty of matches with me," he said with a flash of white teeth.

The road to Cades Cove passed open fields, homesteads, and little frame churches where pioneers had lived almost unnoticed for a century. Then they drove into more isolated country where a churning creek followed the sinuous path of the road. Hushed wilderness and misty mountains were all around them.

Taylor could feel one part of her succumbing to the natural beauty of what she saw even while she reminded herself that it was one thing to appreciate these mountains from the safety of the Blazer and quite another to actually be out in them.

"The leaves haven't changed color as much as I thought they would by now," Adam finally commented.

"Perhaps it's because we haven't had a good frost yet," she ventured.

"Contrary to popular belief, it's the shortening daylight that sets off the chemical reaction, not the advent of frosty nights," he gently corrected. "I think this is our turn up ahead on the left. What does the map show?"

"If this is Abrams Falls, then we're in the right place," she said guardedly as they drove past a trail sign.

Adam turned off the main park road and headed even deeper into the woods. The road was no more than a rough, dirt lane now with giant trees towering overhead on either side and thick brush underneath. Much of the afternoon sun was blotted out by the growth of vegetation, the woods dark and dank all around them. Taylor suddenly had the distinct impression they were entering another world.

The magnitude of what she had done in agreeing to come along on this camping trip finally hit home. She had committed herself to spending two days and two nights in this isolated wilderness with Adam at her side. She had to admit she'd naively envisioned other campers clustered around them, other campfires a welcoming beacon in the dead of night. But they hadn't spotted another tent or a single human being since leaving the main road a few miles back.

Taylor liked to think of herself as a woman of independence. After all, she'd been taking care of herself for a long time now. But out here she was dependent on Adam and that was a circumstance she had failed to foresee. This was his world, not hers. He was the one who felt at home in this godforsaken place—only it wasn't truly godforsaken. It was just the opposite and the artist in her acknowledged that. In a sort of primeval way, it was the most beautiful spot she'd ever seen.

There was something almost seductive about the idea of the two of them out there all alone. Perhaps in this place of magnificent quiet she would be forced to look at the questions she'd managed to avoid asking herself for the past week. It all boiled down to one question in the end. Was she in love with Adam McCord?

"Well, here we are," Adam briskly announced as he pulled the four-wheeler off the road.

Taylor glanced up to see a small, deserted clearing in the middle of a grove of trees. Talk about primeval!

"You mean to tell me that this is it?" She turned and looked at him a little blankly.

"Yep!" Apparently, he failed to see anything amiss.

"Where is everybody?" The words spilled out of her mouth.

"I'm sorry, honey, but there isn't anybody else," Adam apologized unrepentantly. "It's a little late in the season for most campers."

"Obviously—" she muttered dryly.

"Let's get out and stretch our legs. We'll take a look around before we set up camp."

"Do we have to?" She grimaced, suddenly getting cold feet.

"C'mon, Taylor—give it a chance. Who knows? You might even like it." He got out and came around to open the door for her.

"I'm warning you—I don't know the first thing about being in the wilds," she said as he reached up to help her down.

"Well, I do—so stick close!"

Stick close? She didn't intend to let him out of her sight for a minute! And maybe—just maybe that was the way he had planned it all along. She'd always suspected Adam of being the wily type.

"Where do we put the tent?" she politely inquired, permitting herself a small sigh as she tramped along behind him while he studied the campsite from one end to the other. She assumed that was an appropriate question to ask at a time like this.

"We'll pitch the tent right over there," Adam said as he pointed to a small rise in the center of the clearing, "and we'll build our fire here." He indicated a circle of stones apparently left by a previous tenant.

"And where are all the conveniences of home?" Taylor asked, looking around her with a dour expression.

"All the conveniences of home?" he repeated with a puzzled look on his face.

"Yes, you know, hot and cold running water, et cetera."

"Oh—the 'et cetera' is just down the road that way," he laughed, directing her to a small, unpainted outhouse some distance away.

"You don't seriously expect me to use *that*, do you?" she hooted, wondering if it were possible for a twenty-seven-year-old woman in excellent health to suddenly experience heart failure.

"For crying out loud, Jameson, this isn't the damned Hilton!" he roared, out of patience. "In case you hadn't noticed we're out in the middle of nowhere!"

"I was beginning to wonder, *McCord*, if I was the only one who'd noticed that little fact," she shot back, her eyes ablaze. With hands on her hips, she glared at him. "If I told you once, I told you a hundred times I wouldn't be any good at this." She circled around him, gesturing wildly. "But, oh no, you wouldn't listen! Not the high and mighty Lieutenant Adam McCord who always knows what's best for everyone but himself. You insisted on dragging me out here in the middle of God knows where and now you—"

She felt two strong arms shoot out to pull her up against the steel wall of his chest. His face was menacingly close to hers, his breathing as labored as her own. It took Taylor a moment to realize that he was shaking with laughter. "Oh, honey, you are a sight to behold when you get your dander up. We're here now, Taylor, so let's try to make the best of it. If you really want me to I'll take you home first thing in the morning."

His was the voice of reason—to her regret. She rather enjoyed ranting and raving at him. One had so few opportunities for that kind of thing in this civilized age.

Taylor eyed him suspiciously. "If I say go, then we go?"

"I promise."

"All right," she conceded with a sniff, "I suppose I can stick it out for one night."

"Good!" Adam punctuated that with a swift, hard kiss on her lips. "Let's set up camp while there's still some daylight left. I guarantee you'll feel better once we get a fire started and put a pot of coffee on to heat."

With that he circled back to the Blazer and began to unload their supplies from the rear, his muscles flexing under the red-plaid shirt he was wearing.

"Well, what's next on the agenda?" Taylor asked once everything was spread out on the ground around them. It looked like an unholy mess to her.

"The first thing we have to do is get the tent up," Adam told her, swinging the large roll of canvas and poles over his shoulder before striding off toward the rise he had indicated would be its location. "Bring that hatchet with you," he called back to her as she stood there staring after him.

Taylor gingerly picked up the leather-shielded hatchet and followed him. "Now what?" she inquired, watching as he expertly spread the tent out on the ground.

"Now I want you to get inside with the aluminum

frame and hold it up for me while I pull out the guide ropes and pound the stakes into the ground."

She looked at the contraption he had assembled and placed in her hands. "That's all I have to do? Just hold this up in the middle of the tent?" It wasn't heavy, only a little unwieldy in size.

"Yep, once I get the stakes set at each corner, I'll be in to tie up the framework." She had no choice but to take Adam at his word as he held the flap open and guided her inside. "Now hold it up!" She heard him bark through the canvas walls.

"I'm trying to, *sir*," she gritted, finding it was easier said than done. She heard him pounding the stakes in at each corner, and then his large bulk appeared at the opening of the tent.

"You're doing just fine, honey," Adam complimented. He began to relieve her of some of the strain as he tied the frame to the loops in the canvas.

Taylor stepped back outside and viewed the domed tent with satisfaction. "We did it!" She had to admit she was a little surprised by her own success in the matter.

"I always knew you could once you'd made up your mind," Adam claimed, smiling down at her with approval.

Still basking in the warmth of that approval, Taylor hiked back to the mound of supplies and hitched a sleeping bag under each arm. She didn't have to be told they went inside the tent. After a half-hour of diligent work on both their parts, the campsite was beginning to take shape, its orderliness somehow a comfort to her.

"We need to get a fire started if we want to eat tonight," Adam reminded her as he gathered up what she assumed was kindling and stacked it within the circle of rocks. "Think you can handle some of the smaller logs from that woodpile?" he gently challenged, indicating a stack some distance from the campsite.

"Of course, I can," she assured him with a confident smile. "I opened a ketchup bottle for you once. Remember?"

"Much to my embarrassment," he mumbled, putting a match to the kindling.

"Oh, how the mighty have fallen," Taylor murmured as she took off in the direction of the woodpile.

Half a dozen trips later they stood and surveyed the stack of firewood neatly piled a short distance from the circle of rocks. "That should be enough to see us through the evening," Adam said, adding several of the smaller logs to the growing fire. "Why don't you take a seat while I start our dinner?" He thoughtfully spread a tarp on the ground for her.

"Thank you." She suddenly realized she was both tired and thirsty. "Could I have something to drink while the coffee water heats?"

"Sure, there's some canned soda in the cooler I brought, but remember if you want water only drink what we brought with us. We can use water from the pump for dishes and bathing once we've boiled it, but it's still safer to drink only from the tank," he warned, referring to the water stored in the rear of the Blazer. "We'll have to keep all our food and water in the four-wheeler at night, too."

Taylor arched a brow in question. "Why not put that stuff in the tent?"

"Well, for one thing there's not enough room, and for another it might attract animals. We don't want any nocturnal visitors disturbing our sleep. We'll have to dispose of our garbage carefully for the same reason. One thing about bears and raccoons, they're great scavengers."

"Bears and raccoons?" she echoed, furtively staring into the nearby woods.

"Don't worry. They're a lot more afraid of you than you are of them," Adam soothed in a confident tone.

"You have no idea what a comfort that is to me." Taylor shivered, hugging herself. "I think I'll get my jacket. Do you want anything?"

Adam looked up at her from his hunched position over the campfire, his gaze following the line of her leg from ankle to thigh. "Ah, no, I don't want anything," he muttered as if he were biting his tongue.

Taylor retrieved her windbreaker from the tent with a minimum of fuss, trying to avoid looking around its close confines or thinking ahead to the night, when they would be sleeping there together. She wasn't going to think about that now, she told herself as she returned to the campfire. She settled herself cross-legged on the tarp and watched as Adam deftly wrapped their meat and vegetables in heavy foil before placing the packets on hot stones near the coals.

"How can you be so handy out here and tell me you're all thumbs in the kitchen?" she wondered aloud as he worked.

"I guess it doesn't seem the same out here," he admitted, getting to his feet. "Nothing seems the same out here to me," he added thoughtfully. "How about a cold beer?"

Taylor suddenly remembered how thirsty she was.

"I'd love a cold beer," she was surprised to hear herself reply. Normally, she didn't care for its bitter taste, but right now a beer sounded delicious.

Adam sauntered over to the Blazer and came back with a can of beer in each hand. He set one down while he flipped the tab on the other and handed it to her.

"Thanks," she said, tearing her gaze from him as he sat down beside her on the tarp, his shoulder inadvertently bumping against hers.

They sat there in companionable silence, sipping their beer, watching the gathering shadows of dusk as darkness descended on the woods surrounding the campsite. Taylor had to admit that it was incredibly peaceful there. Little wonder a man like Adam loved these mountains and woods. There was a sense of something far bigger than one human being and his problems in the sweeping grandeur of the place. It had taken a thousand millenniums for these mountains and valleys to form. What was the span of a man's life compared to that?

The forest exuded a scent of damp pine needles and autumn foliage that mingled with the natural fragrance of burning wood and the tantalizing aroma of their dinner cooking on the coals. All of this was larger than life, and yet sitting there beside Adam, gazing into the glowing embers, it was somehow cozy and intimate as well. Taylor was surprised to hear herself sigh with a genuine sense of contentment. She'd never expected to admit it even to herself, but she was glad she had come.

This was indeed a world away from her apartment in Knoxville or even Adam's with its clutter of newspapers and books. "I was thinking of bringing the Dashiell Hammett novel with me," she finally offered in a quiet voice that somehow seemed appropriate in this very quiet place, "but I can see now that I wouldn't have done much reading, anyway." She sat back and dreamily stared into the flickering flames of the campfire.

"I always think I'll study when I come up here, but I never even open a book," Adam echoed, content to lean back against the oversized log behind them.

"What do you study?" she murmured sleepily. "All those law books with the fancy titles I saw on the shelf in your apartment?"

Taylor felt him stiffen beside her. "I wasn't aware that you had even noticed," he said in a guarded tone.

She proceeded with infinite care, suddenly aware that she had hit a sensitive nerve. "Are you studying law, Adam?" she gently prodded.

"I've been doing a little on my own," he admitted, nonchalantly taking a drink of his beer.

She picked up a small stick and began to draw circles in the dirt at their feet. "Do you have plans to do more than a little?"

"I'd like to go to law school," he said, his mouth twisting into a wry smile, "but I guess we all have our pipe dreams."

Taylor looked up at him, her eyes widening expressively. "Why does it have to be only a pipe dream? I think you'd make a wonderful lawyer."

"Maybe—but it takes two things I don't have," he said, staring into the campfire. "Time and money."

For a minute or two, Taylor was at a genuine loss for words. If it had been within her power to wave some magic wand and grant this man his wish, she would have done so in an instant. As it was, her respect and admiration for Adam suddenly grew by leaps and bounds. He was a dedicated police officer. That she knew. But to think that while he held down a difficult job with long hours he was also studying law on his own said a great deal about him and his sense of determination.

"How long have you been studying on your own?" she asked at last.

"A year or two," Adam replied vaguely, getting up to check on the progress of their dinner.

"Have you always been interested in becoming a lawyer?" she asked, her curiosity aroused.

"No—not really," he admitted somewhat begrudgingly.

"Then what got you interested in law as a profession?" she persisted, sensing that he was holding something back from her.

He gave a short, dry laugh. "I've been a policeman for ten years, honey. Isn't that reason enough?"

"Perhaps," she said in a quiet, but firm voice, "but not every policeman wants to become a lawyer. I think you know that as well as I do." Her eyes sought his over the top of the campfire, refusing to relinquish their hold once she had his attention.

"Yes, I know," he muttered, dropping his gaze under her scrutiny. He ran a relentless hand through his hair. "You just won't let up, will you?" He looked up and met her unwavering gaze.

"No, I won't," she said hoarsely, then nearly relented when she glimpsed the look in his eyes. "Adam—"

He stopped her with a single gesture. "My best

friend was killed a little more than two years ago," he said in a quiet voice. "He was my partner and I watched him die."

"Oh, dear God . . ." she murmured, but neither of them paid the slightest heed to her prayer.

Once he had told her that much Adam seemed determined to go on. "It took me a while to get over Brad's death. Hell, it was weeks, maybe months before I could begin to accept the fact that he was dead at all." He paused and stared into the fire. "A cop has to face the fact that life and death are a part of his job, but it was never the same for me after that. When the case went to court I was called as a material witness. That's when I began to realize that justice could be served in more ways than one by the right kind of man. I guess that's when the idea of studying law started in the back of my mind."

"That must have been just before you moved to Knoxville," Taylor whispered, scarcely daring to breathe.

Adam nodded his head. "After the case was tried I took off by myself for a couple of weeks and came down here to the Smoky Mountains. I kind of put it all back together while I was out here. When I got back to Pittsburgh I knew I was all right again, but I wanted a change. This seemed to be the logical place." He shrugged and turned his attention to their dinner. Then as if sensing that her eyes were still on him, he looked up again. "It's all right, honey. Honestly, it is. I worked it out a long time ago."

Taylor blinked back the tears. It was too late for tears now. She gazed from the woods to the shadowy mountains on the horizon to the immense night sky beyond and knew he was telling her the truth. She had been right about this place. She was suddenly grateful that all of this had been here for him when he had needed it so.

"Well, I think we'd better eat before our dinner burns to a crisp," Adam announced briskly, removing the foil packets from the fire.

Taylor sensed the change in his mood and altered hers accordingly. "I'm absolutely starved!" she boldly lied. "You forgot to tell me what camping in the great outdoors does to your appetite."

All of a sudden he was innocence itself. "Yep, you can really work up an appetite out here. That's for sure."

She nearly dropped the tin plates she was handing him when she glimpsed the less than innocent sparkle in his eyes. "In that case," she said rather too sweetly, "perhaps the cook had better dish up the food."

They filled their plates and settled down around the campfire to eat. Taylor was surprised to find herself gulping down every bite. "This is delicious," she told him sincerely.

"Naturally," Adam remarked with a slightly indignant look. "Did you honestly expect anything less from a Boy Scout?"

"And do you live by the scout motto as well?" she goaded, her mouth curving upward in a shameless grin.

A slow, sardonic smile appeared on Adam's face. "I've always been *prepared* and don't you doubt it for a minute, my dear Taylor."

She was totally disconcerted for a moment. "I-ah-I think I'll rinse the dishes while the water is nice and hot." She scrambled to her feet and busied herself with cleaning up the plates and forks they had used. It was some ten minutes later before she was ready to face him again. "There's just enough hot water left for each of us to take a 'spit' bath. Do you mind if I go first?"

Adam took a pack of cigarettes from his shirt pocket and lit one, slowly exhaling before he answered. "I'll be glad to make myself scarce for a few minutes, but wouldn't you like to use the 'conveniences' before you get undressed?"

She wrinkled up her nose in distaste. "I don't suppose there's any way to avoid it."

He merely smiled and shrugged. "I'll get you the flashlight."

Taylor returned to the campsite some time later, grumbling under her breath. She rammed the flashlight back in Adam's hand. "*Now* you can make yourself scarce."

Once she was certain he was leaning against the Blazer with his back to her, she took the small pan of hot water over by the tent. She took off her jacket and blouse and quickly washed herself the best she could before slipping out of her jeans. Just as quickly she slipped into her pajamas. There was nothing seductive about freezing to death in the nude! With the windbreaker clutched around her, Taylor stepped away from the tent and disposed of the pan of water.

She draped her washcloth and towel over one of the tent ropes and turned to call out to Adam, only to discover that he was standing right behind her.

"Don't sneak up on me like that!" she snapped at him. "You scared me half out of my wits."

"Sorry." But he didn't sound the least bit apologetic as he plucked the small pan from her grasp. "And just how do you intend to make *yourself* scarce?"

"I suppose you could let me borrow one of your cigarettes?" she retorted rather caustically.

He shook his head. "Nasty habit, smoking."

Taylor flung up a defiant chin. "I could always promise to keep my eyes closed."

At that he really laughed, still shaking his head. "The temptation might prove to be too great even for you." The color rushed to her cheeks. Her mouth started to work, but no sound came out. "Why don't you just stay in the tent?" he finally suggested. "There are only a couple of things left that need to be put in the Blazer. I'll wash up outside. I can always use the water to douse the fire. I'll be back in a minute," he said while she scurried inside.

For heaven's sake, Taylor thought, she was behaving like a hysterical schoolgirl. Well, she'd be damned if Adam would come back and find her cowering in her sleeping bag! It was time to face the facts. She was a normal, healthy, twenty-seven-year-old female who was about to spend the night alone with a *very* normal, healthy male. There was no mistaking the look in Adam's eyes tonight. He wanted her. And if she were honest she had to admit that she wanted him as well. Oh, how she wanted him! What could seem more natural than to seek that exquisite satisfaction they could find in each other's arms beneath the stars?

She impatiently pulled the bandana from her hair, letting it fall around her shoulders in a shower of silvery gold dust. Long, languid strokes with a brush left it a shimmering mass that would entice any man to run his fingers through its softness. Slipping out of her hiking boots and socks, Taylor unzipped the sleeping bag and got in, lying there quietly listening to the night—the hoot of a distant owl, the restless wind tossing the treetops to and fro overhead, the faint but unmistakable sounds of Adam moving about the campsite.

Suddenly, she understood that Adam had always been the question and the answer in one. The question wasn't whether she wanted to sleep with a man, but with *this* man. The answer was simple. Tonight she would love him, love him with everything that she was, give to him freely of that love, and tomorrow— tomorrow would have to take care of itself. That was all anyone could ask or expect. Tomorrow held no promise of its own. There was only this night and what it would bring.

She heard the hiss of water hitting hot coals and then there was only the hush of darkness all around. Her heart was hammering wildly in her breast, but not from fear. For out there in the darkness was the one man who with his kiss and his touch could ignite a far greater flame within her. She lay there, waiting, hearing the soft fall of his footsteps as he approached the tent.

There was the distinctive sound of the flap being unzipped and then Taylor saw Adam's looming form as he ducked his head and came into the tent. She could make out the shirt he carried in one hand, the flashlight in the other, and his bare chest only inches away. She could smell the slight odor of burning wood and smoke that clung to him, the damp pine that mingled with his own masculine scent.

He tossed the shirt and flashlight aside and stretched out on the sleeping bag next to hers, turning toward her. "Are you asleep?" came his whispered query.

He was joking, of course, but it seemed neither of

them found it humorous. "No—I'm not asleep," she whispered back.

"It hasn't been as bad as you thought it would be, has it?" Adam gently prompted, bringing his face closer.

She could feel the watchfulness in him. It was there in his shadowed face, in the taut pose of his body as he leaned over her.

"No." Her voice sounded strangely foreign to her own ears. "It hasn't been as bad as I thought."

Then Adam brought his mouth down to hers, his breathing oddly sporadic as he lightly brushed his lips across it, his fingers momentarily losing themselves in the velvety softness of her hair.

"So soft, so damnably sweet," he marveled. Taylor found she could scarcely breathe, much less speak. She desperately wanted to reach out and wrap her arms about him, but they seemed to be frozen to her sides. He kissed her again, asking for no display of passion and giving none. "Good night, Taylor," he said quietly, disentangling himself.

She felt his warmth taken from her and mourned its loss. She heard the gentle scraping of his jeans against the sleeping bag. She watched in silence as he turned on his side, his back toward her.

Surely it wasn't going to end like this? With a dispassionate kiss and a casual good night? She listened as Adam's breathing became more regular, cursing the sleep that suddenly seemed to elude only one of them.

Damn the man, he'd done it to her again! Just when she'd finally made up her mind she could make the commitment that he wanted, he wasn't asking it of her. He was the one who was always complaining it was never the right time or place. And he was the one who had arrogantly claimed that sooner or later they would make love. Dammit! Then why wasn't that time now and the place here?

In frustration she turned away from him and stared into the darkness. Oh, God, she hurt like hell! She wanted Adam so badly she could almost taste it. She longed for the touch, the kiss that could make her forget everything and everyone but this man. She despaired for the sweet oblivion she knew could be found in his arms. She didn't want to lie there thinking the night away. She wanted only to *feel*.

Yes, indeed, how the mighty had fallen. In this quivering mass of human emotions, who would recognize the dignified and very proper Taylor Jameson? She could intellectualize all she wanted to about reason ruling emotion. But she had discovered she was a woman of emotion first, last and foremost. And she wanted to prove that fact to Adam beyond a shadow of a doubt. She wanted to be enough of a woman to bring out the man in him: the man who would tremble in her embrace; the man who would hunger for her kiss, her caress; the man who would gladly lose himself in the mindless wonder of her body.

She wanted to be so close to him that they became one body with one heart beating for them both, one desire driving them to seek its satisfaction in each other. She wanted to feel him all around her, through her, in her. She wanted to know this man's heart and body and soul as no one else ever had or ever would again. She had never played the role of aggressor, but perhaps the time had come for her to take fate in her hands and determine the course of her own future.

Taylor felt the breath catch in her throat as the man beside her stirred. Then she heard the zipper being worked on the tent door. She had thought Adam was asleep. Apparently, she'd been wrong.

She turned over and put her hand out to discover that his sleeping bag was empty. Quietly moving to the front of the tent, she peered out into the darkness. At first, she couldn't see Adam anywhere. Then he struck a match, its brief light revealing his tall figure some distance away. He was standing there, the faint glow of his cigarette visible as it moved from his mouth down to his side and back up again.

It seemed that sleep was eluding them both after all. Taylor knew then that she would go to him. Without stopping to consider the wisdom of her actions, she unzipped the flap and stepped outside, her bare feet making no sound in the soft dirt. She was almost directly behind him before she said his name.

"Adam . . ." She saw him start as he jerked around, the expression on his face nearly enough to make her turn and run.

"I thought you were asleep," he muttered, taking a long draw on the cigarette.

"I thought *you* were asleep," she countered in a husky voice.

"I felt like having a cigarette," he admitted in a low-pitched rumble. "I couldn't seem to sleep anyway."

"Aren't you cold out here dressed like that?" Surely he must be. From all appearances he was wearing only a pair of jeans.

"No, I'm not cold. You'd better go back inside now, Taylor." His tone was uncompromising, his displeasure apparent.

"Adam, I-I hope it isn't something I've done," she began, then stammered to a halt. "What I mean is I hope I didn't stir up unhappy memories for you earlier tonight."

He uttered a growling profanity. Then with uncharacteristic violence he threw the cigarette to the ground and crushed it under his bare foot.

"Adam!" She started to bend over him.

"Dammit, Taylor! Let it be!"

Her eyes were two large pools of concern. "But you're hurt. . . ."

"If I am it has nothing to do with a damned silly burn," he softly raged. "If I can't sleep it's not because of any unhappy memories you might have stirred up." He drove his fingers through his hair in a gesture of frustration. "Don't you understand, honey? It's you. It's all you!"

Her mouth formed his name, but no sound was forthcoming. She reached out and encountered the muscled wall of his chest, the surprisingly soft curls that ran riot down his torso. Her hand was caught between them as Adam crushed her against him.

His eyes burned into hers. "I need for you to be there, Taylor."

This time she answered him without hesitation. "I am, Adam. I am!"

7

Taylor felt the tension in him like a tautly drawn bow string about to snap.

"Are you sure?" Adam rasped, barely controlling the harshness in his voice. "Are you very sure?"

"I've never been more sure of anything in my life," she declared, burying her face in the soft mat of hair in the center of his chest, her nails gently digging into his bare skin.

"It seems like I've been waiting a lifetime to hear you say that," he growled, the tension slowly ebbing from him, only to be replaced by another kind of tension. His hands began to move compulsively up and down her back as if he needed to prove to himself that she was flesh and blood and not merely some figment of his imagination.

Taylor looked up at him, meeting head-on her own

desire reflected there in his eyes. She freed her hands, going up on tiptoe to entwine them about his neck.

"I want you, Adam McCord." It was spoken in a quiet voice, but there was no doubt that she meant what she said, and somehow in saying it aloud the barriers between them began to softly crumble.

She touched her lips to his like a gentle rainshower falling on parched ground, lightly feathering her caress across each strongly defined feature of his face before finding the pulsating cord at the side of his neck and lingering there.

"God knows I want you, Taylor," he proclaimed in husky tones, his hands delving beneath the silky material to encircle her waist. His touch was pleasantly cool on her heated skin. "So soft and slender, so invitingly sweet in my hands." His murmur became a groan. "I want you so damned much, honey, I'm half afraid I might hurt you!"

"Adam, I'm a woman, not a china doll," she reassured him.

Suddenly, as if the extra adrenaline flowing through his veins gave him added strength, he picked her up off the ground until she was face to face with him.

"I'm a man who wants you the way a man wants his woman," he gritted with unmistakable intent.

"And I want you the way a woman wants her man," she chorused, running her fingers down the expanse of his bare chest until he rewarded her with a slight shudder.

He was like a hot, scorching wind that tore the breath from her lungs. His tongue surged between her teeth to plunder the moist interior of her mouth. Her pajamas proved to be of little consequence between them as she was crushed to his chest. The night chill had already brought her nipples to erect peaks that teased him through her clothing.

She caressed his chest and back, marveling at the paradox of smooth flesh and hard muscle, wondering at the strength in his arms and shoulders, the leanness of his waist and above all her own driving need to know every inch of this man. She touched him, and for a moment her heart stood still. There was something fearfully masculine about him. Like Samson of old, there was some mystery to his strength which she couldn't begin to understand.

Adam slipped his hands behind her, his fingernails lightly scoring the tender flesh through the material of her pajamas. He cupped her rounded bottom in his grasp and urged her closer and closer to his own growing insistency. Then he eased his hands beneath the elastic waistband and found himself imprisoned between the silky material and her equally silky skin.

Taylor clutched the back pockets of his jeans for support, holding on for dear life as he traced a sensuous line down the narrow valley that dipped between the two soft mounds. Then his touch moved lower to find her with the tip of his finger, eliciting an immediate response from her body. A response she had never dreamt possible.

"Adam?" She was suddenly afraid, uncertain.

"Don't be afraid, darling," he soothed as he gently fondled her. "I want all the sweet responses your lovely body has to give."

He tentatively probed her secret places, her natural responses moistening his hand. Then he drove deeper, bringing forth a cry from her that broke the silence of the night. He swallowed the sound, his tongue thrusting between her parted lips in that other imitation of the ultimate act of love between a man and a woman.

Her head moved back and forth beneath his, her whimpers filling his mouth, mingling with his own groaning need until she was certain she would go mad with wanting him.

"Taylor, if we don't stop I'm going to lay you down in the grass and make love to you here and now," he threatened in a strangely hoarse voice.

"I want to love you, Adam," she whispered frantically, wild with the mindless desires that chained her to him.

He gently withdrew his hand and looked down at her, his eyes dark and smoldering with need. "It's too cold out here, honey. Let's go inside the tent," he urged, leading her in that direction.

She placed her hand in his and followed, pausing as he zipped the canvas door closed behind them, the night breeze wafting through the mesh opening. Then Adam knelt before her on the cushion of their sleeping bags and drew her down to her knees. His arms went around her as he kissed her with a heartrending tenderness.

"I want to love you, Taylor."

"Yes, Adam," she vowed, meeting his kiss with one of her own.

He reached out and carefully undid each satin-covered button down the front of her pajamas. The top was eased off her shoulders and down her arms until she knelt before him nude to the waist. For a moment he could only look at her. The pale moonlight filtered into the tent, revealing her silky white breasts and their pink-tinged tips. Almost with reverence he raised his hands to cup their fullness, vowing to himself that he would not rush the wonderful discovery that was about to take place between them.

He supported the weight of both breasts in his hands, his thumbs circling the rosy peaks. Delicately fingering one nipple, he watched in fascination as it responded, a hard bud in a circle of softness. Then he bent his head and touched her with the tip of his tongue, flicking it back and forth across the painfully taut nipple that seemed to beg him for more, always for more.

He moved to the other, his hair teasing the sensitized skin between her breasts as his mouth languorously trailed back and forth between them. Taylor caught his head in her hands, cradling him between her splayed fingers, holding him to her as he finally took pity on her. He suckled at one breast, his hand fingering the other until her head fell back and a low moan issued forth through her parted teeth.

He nipped at her, erotically tugged at her, darted with an audacious tongue between her breasts, his caresses hot and moist on her skin. The night was all around them, the wind whistling through the trees, and yet nothing existed for them outside that one small enclosure.

When she thought she could humanly stand no more Taylor insistently nudged him away and began to explore all the wonders of his body with loving hands and mouth and tongue. She delighted in the distinctive taste of him, tangy and slightly salty. She inhaled the fragrance of his skin, reveling in it.

Her teeth nibbled at his flat brown nipples, the curve of his shoulder, the tender lobe of an ear until he was trembling under her erotic assault as surely as she had under his.

Her hands slid down the passion-slick skin of his chest to settle momentarily at his waist. Her nails scraped the smooth abdomen, the line of his hip, the sinewy muscle of his thigh in a tantalizing gesture. She took a deep breath and daringly moved her hand to stroke the indisputable evidence of his desire. She heard his sharp intake of air, felt his body respond to the stimulus of her caress as he pressed boldly against her.

She found the snap at his waist, and eased the zipper down with infinite care once she confirmed that he truly wore nothing underneath. She trailed her fingers through the small patch of hair that curled about his navel and then lower.

"Oh, God, Taylor!" Adam groaned her name from deep within as he laid her back on the sleeping bag, his hands moving over her with a trembling but sure touch.

He tugged at the elastic waistband, easing her pajamas down her thighs and finally tossing them aside. She lay there fully vulnerable to his gaze and his caress. His passion barely held in check, he impatiently pulled the jeans down his hips and flung them away. Then he was beside her at last, bare skin to bare skin.

Somehow it seemed the most natural thing in the world for her to appreciate all that he now was. "You're—you're beautiful," she whispered in awe, gazing at his man's body stretched out beside her.

"And you're the loveliest thing I've ever seen," he said in hushed tones, his caress a gentle breeze on her skin like the night air that softly blew through the tent.

She reciprocated in kind, letting her fingers roam down his side and along his leg, circling back to his thighs. "I-I never knew a man's skin could be so soft," she murmured in dreamy wonderment.

"Dear God, do you have any idea what you do to me?" Adam fiercely breathed against her mouth.

"I know what you do to me," she softly confessed, her body on fire for him, hungering for him in some elemental, female way.

His fingers lovingly stroked her, soothing the rapid rise and fall of her breasts, trailing a random pattern across the smooth expanse of her abdomen before descending to find the core of her femininity in a light caress. At her instinctive response he delved deeper, parting her flesh, finding her warm and moist and welcoming. She arched against his hand, her body driven into his as his teeth closed around her taut nipple.

"Adam—please, love me! Love me now!" she cried out, the madness he was creating in her more than she could bear.

"Yes, yes, now!" he agreed huskily, parting her legs, but it was not as she had imagined it would be.

He lowered his head to kiss the creamy hollow between her breasts and then the curve of a rounded hip and finally the sensitive skin of her inner thigh. His mouth was warm against her even greater warmth until she was a mass of quivering flesh beneath his onslaught.

"Please, Adam!" His name was a plea on her lips as she groped for him, seeking that elusive satisfaction she sensed that he and he alone could give her.

"Yes, darling, now!" he promised as he stretched his body above hers, settling himself between her thighs.

Probing gently at first, he completed the union

between them, making their flesh now one. For a moment all was still as the full import of that union was realized and then he began to move, swaying against her before his control slipped away and he drove with greater force as she adjusted to his ultimate claim on her. They found their natural rhythm together, spinning out of control until Taylor felt an exquisite pressure building within her, threatening to explode.

"No! No!" She mindlessly shook her head from side to side, suddenly afraid to go where it seemed he would not follow.

"Yes, darling! I want it all! I want all of your passion!" he urged as the search took him into her again, sending her over the edge, hurling her into the void of darkest space. But she was no longer afraid for his soft love words followed her, reassured her, and in the end smoothed her way back to him.

He was still for a long moment, studying her lovely features as they softened in repose. Then he began to move, slowly at first and then with increasing frenzy as he drove his flesh and hers to the limit. She felt the wondrous pressure building once more and knew that she would die little death after little death there in his arms until he joined her in that final moment when their voices would cry out as one.

Adam took them to the edge again and again until they were both mindless with the sensations they aroused in each other. He was her whole world—the earth beneath and the sky overhead, the deepest ocean and the soaring mountaintop. He was all around her and through her and in her such as she had never known could be. There was no way to describe this miracle that was happening between them.

Taylor became impatient to feel him soar toward that peak she had reached so many times, lifting her hips to thrust against him, moving beneath him with an age-old instinct that worked its madness now as it always had.

"Taylor!" His hoarse cry of ecstasy rang out, telling her that she had succeeded.

And then she fell victim to her own scheme. "Adam!" His name was but a whisper on her lips, but in her mind it was joyously shouted from mountaintop to mountaintop, the sound of it echoing through her, becoming a part of every cell and nerve and particle of her being.

Those long, quiet moments in each other's arms were moments to be savored as well. To lie there in the mindless aftermath of loving, to feel the subtle changes that returned them to reality. To know that passion such as theirs was rare indeed, that trust truly given and received bound them together more irrefutably than any physical union ever could.

He murmured soft, incoherent words against her skin, the slightest touch thrilling her love-sensitized body. At last Adam released her from his weight, rolling to lie beside her, reluctant to let her go. He pulled the sleeping bag around them and, feeling warm and secure within its cocoon and each other's arms, they drifted off to sleep. A sleep without dreams —for them all dreams had come true.

Sometime in the night Taylor briefly stirred, discovering that Adam had drawn the sleeping bags together, one beneath them and the other covering them. She snuggled back down beside him, seeking the warmth and comfort of his body as her eyes closed once again.

She wasn't sure just what woke her. She only knew in some small recess of her mind that she didn't want to awaken. Then it came again, a warm touch on her body as she struggled out of sleep, trying to find the source of the sensations starting to go through her. Her eyes fluttered open to behold the gray light of approaching dawn, to hear the first stirrings of life in the woods around them, to know that Adam was beside her, his hand languorously moving on her stomach.

She wondered if he was caressing her unconsciously as he slept or if he, too, was caught in that nether world between wakefulness and sleep. She turned her head and watched as his eyes slowly flickered open. For a moment neither spoke. Then the edges of Adam's mouth curled up into a warm, lazy smile.

"You're gorgeous in the morning," he mumbled in a sleep-rusty voice, his hand continuing to trace infuriating little circles on her stomach.

"So are you," she murmured shyly, sucking in her breath when his hand moved lower to shape the curve of her hip, to skim the hollow below her navel.

"Last night I knew for the first time what it was to make love," Adam told her, his eyes going dark with unspoken emotion. "I wanted to tell you then, but we both fell asleep before I could." He moved closer, his mouth hovering above hers, his body no longer slowed by the inertia of sleep.

"Adam?" Taylor felt mild surprise. Although his movements were subtle, his intent was clear. He eased his body onto hers, his weight pressing her down into the cushion of the sleeping bag. He nuzzled her neck just below her ear, taking little nibbles of her tender flesh.

"Let me tell you now, my darling, in the best way I know how," he murmured in a seductive drawl.

He didn't wait for her answer as he brushed his lips along her bare shoulder, sending an involuntary shiver through her body. Then his mouth fastened to hers as his hands slid under her to cup her hips. He pressed her up into him, thrilling her with his totally arrogant male need.

"Adam, you're crushing me. I-I can't breathe," she gasped, feeling her traitorous body already responding to him.

He propped himself up on his elbows and stared down into her eyes, then grunted, apparently satisfied with what he saw there, knowing that she wanted him, too. He eased his weight from her slender form and rolled over, taking her with him as he tossed the covers aside. Taylor was stunned for a moment to find herself sprawled across his chest, her body covering his.

"Now I'm not crushing you," he pointed out with a smug little smile. A smile that quickly faded as he studied the lovely form poised above him.

Despite his heated gaze, the chill morning air caused her to shiver. "Th-That was sneaky," she chattered through her teeth.

"You're cold," he said with concern, reaching for the red-plaid shirt he'd carelessly discarded the night before. He held it up as she slipped into the oversized garment, then rolled the sleeves up past her wrists.

Taylor took her eyes off him as she reached down to do up the buttons, inhaling the scent of him, which lingered on the shirt. But Adam grasped her hands in one of his, stilling her movements, putting a stop to her efforts.

"No, darling, no," he murmured, his other hand

parting the front of the shirt. "I want to see you when we make love this time."

He ran his hands over her smooth skin, looking up into her passion-glazed eyes. Her body seemed to be stretched above his in offering. He reached up to caress the tip of her breast, then gently urged her toward him until the hardening peak was pressed to his lips. He kissed it tenderly, worshipfully. He groaned aloud and took it into his mouth, his tongue wrapping around the taut bud. Then he drew her closer, enfolding her in his arms as he found her mouth in a long, drugging kiss.

Taylor clung to him, her fingers digging into his shoulders as his hands traveled beneath the shirt to warm her. He trailed a fiery path from her nape to the rounded curves of her hips. Then his touch became more insistent, reaching every sensitive area of her body, exciting her to a level of desire that left her trembling.

Adam's breathing became harsh, his touch a torment as he shifted his hips under her and drew her down onto him. A wave of shock coursed through them both as their bodies met and joined as one.

Her eyes flew open. "Adam, I-I can't! I don't know what to do," she confessed in a frenzied whisper.

"You can, honey. I'll show you," he assured her, his hands settling on her hips as he began to move beneath her, movements that quickly caught them both up in the rhythmic cadence of love.

He thrust deeper as they reached together for that mindless oblivion, that moment when nothing else existed but the passionate pleasure they gave to each other. They rushed forward to meet that moment as one, clinging to one another as they scaled the dizzying heights. For a brief moment in time, they gazed down at the world from that pinnacle and then together began the slow descent back to earth.

For a long time—neither could have said how long—they lay there without speaking, without moving. There were no more words now, only the utter contentment, the complete fulfillment they had found in each other's arms. When Taylor stirred at last it was to look down into Adam's face with the all-encompassing love she felt for him plain in her eyes.

"I don't understand," she confessed in a small voice as she curled against his side. "I never knew it could be like this."

Adam turned his head and gazed down at her, his sculpted features softened by the same emotions he saw written on hers. "I can't begin to explain it," he sighed, holding her close to him. "Perhaps there are some things that simply can't be explained."

Minutes passed before she chose to speak again. "Look—the sun is coming up. It's morning."

"I promised to take you home this morning if you wanted to go," Adam reminded her with obvious reluctance. "Do you want to go, Taylor?" His eyes were momentarily shadowed with doubt.

"No, Adam, I don't," she proclaimed, speaking from her heart and not her head.

"I have a feeling this weekend is going to be the best damned weekend of my entire life," he cheerfully declared. "In fact, all of a sudden I'm ravenous!"

"So what's new?" she teased, finding his lighthearted mood contagious.

Adam pushed himself up into a sitting position, his

eyes bright and clear, his tone humorous. "Woman, I am going to make you the breakfast of your life. Have you ever eaten flapjacks cooked over an open fire?"

At that she laughed. "You know I haven't."

"Then you're in for a real treat." He bounced to his feet with a grin and started pulling his jeans on. "C'mon, honey, up and at it!"

"I suppose we'll need more logs from the woodpile if we're going to have that 'open fire.'" She groaned, rubbing her shoulder as if she'd just remembered how sore her muscles were.

"It'll be worth the effort," he promised, balancing himself on one foot as he pulled a sock on. "Trust me."

It turned out he was right on both counts—the flapjacks were worth the effort and it was the best weekend of both their lives. All too soon it was Sunday afternoon and they were breaking camp in preparation for their return to Knoxville. Adam was loading the tent in the back of the Blazer while Taylor gathered up the last of their things.

He stopped and took out a cigarette, leaning back against the four-wheeler to watch her as he inhaled slowly. He stood there, contemplative, staring into space, the cigarette forgotten in his hand.

Taylor looked up and saw the slight scowl on his face, but wisely kept silent. Perhaps Adam had the same feeling as she—a genuine reluctance, a kind of wistful sadness at leaving this place, these mountains. She was leaving a part of herself behind, but she was taking something of this place away with her as well. It was more than an even exchange to her way of thinking. For in her heart she knew she would never be quite the same again.

Suddenly, Adam threw his cigarette to the ground, crushing it beneath the heel of his boot as he strode toward her. "I am a total jackass!" he burst out, grabbing the coffeepot from her unsuspecting hands.

"Well, I wouldn't put it that strongly. After all, you've done far more than your share of the work this weekend as it is. I can finish putting these few things away."

He waved her objections aside with a motion of his hand. "No, no, you don't understand! I-I was standing there thinking about how much I love watching you— every movement you make. The way you hold your head. The curve of that cute little rear of yours." She blushed just as he had known she would. "The way you stick out your chin when you're really determined. And then it hit me!" He slapped his forehead in a gesture of self-disgust, his voice softening. "I'm a jackass, my darling Taylor, for not realizing that I love to watch you because I'm in love with you." Adam's voice trailed off on a husky note. He gently raised his hand to her mouth. "And the reason you're doing all of this isn't because you've decided you love camping, but because you love me. . . ." For a moment all she could hear was the thundering beat of her own heart. "You do love me, don't you?" he whispered softly.

Taylor looked up at him and knew that the moment of truth had finally come. "Yes, Adam, I love you," she said simply, but her heart took flight, soaring above the mountain peaks that surrounded them. Dear Lord, he loved her! Adam loved her!

"Thank God!" he intoned, tossing the coffeepot aside without a second thought as he gathered her to him. He simply held her in his arms for a minute, keeping her close to his heart, knowing that his heart was now in her care. Then he raised her mouth to his and kissed her with such exquisite tenderness that the tears sprang to her eyes. "This will always be our special place," he vowed, taking in the isolated campsite, sun-dappled woods and the misty mountains on the horizon. "No matter who comes after us, this place will always be ours."

As they drove away later that afternoon Taylor wistfully looked back at the small clearing in the woods. "Let's come back here again—soon," she sighed, placing her hand in Adam's. Then she turned and looked ahead down the road in front of them.

8

〜〜〜〜〜〜〜〜〜

The next few weeks were the happiest of Taylor's life. She was loved and in love. Autumn had always seemed a rather sad time to her, an ending instead of a beginning, but now she luxuriated in the crisp golden days that finally came to Knoxville as October's vivid scarlets became November's russet-browns.

It was just after two o'clock on a Friday afternoon when she turned the key in the lock and let herself in the front door of the townhouse at 24 Kenton Place. She shoved the cello case in its usual place in the hall closet and laid her briefcase down on the table, finally freeing a hand to grab the small bundle of letters she'd temporarily tucked under her chin.

She dropped her leather shoulder bag on a chair as she went through to the kitchen to put a kettle of water on for her afternoon cup of tea. Quickly sorting through the mail, she tossed the bills in a kitchen drawer expressly set aside for that purpose. She read through the newsy letter from her parents and then came to the last envelope, noting rather curiously that the return address was Chicago.

She slit the envelope open and unfolded the single sheet of official-looking bond and quickly read down the page. Then she read it a second and a third time. She squeezed her eyes tightly shut and then opened them again. The letter was indeed very real and still there in her hands.

What a strange sensation to hold the entire future in her hands, the culmination of years of intense study and hard work. She saw the goal she had aspired to there within her grasp. It was all there in the single-spaced, politely worded request that she join the Chicago Symphony Orchestra as principal cellist at the conclusion of the current season in Knoxville.

This was it, Taylor told herself. This was what it felt like to see a dream come true. She wasn't sure she believed it even now. Yes, she had the credentials. She had even played with the Chicago Symphony a number of times as a guest artist. Yes, she had worked long and hard for this moment and yet, to *hope* and to actually *have* were two entirely different things.

Only a few short weeks ago her initial impulse would have been to telephone her parents with the good news. Now she knew the first person she must share this with was Adam. She picked up the telephone to call him and then halfway through dialing his number put the receiver back down. She suddenly realized she wanted to tell him this kind of momentous news in person.

With the letter still in her hand, she turned off the stove, grabbed her handbag and flew out the door.

She was pulling into a parking space outside his apartment building before she even thought to ask herself if he would be home. Then remembering that he had worked the "graveyard" shift the night before, she knew he might well be. As if to confirm her speculation, she spotted his gray sedan parked a short distance away.

She hurried into the building and took the elevator straight to the fourth floor. Pressing the doorbell of his apartment, she stood back and waited, tapping her foot impatiently. When that brought no response she tried again. This time she heard someone stirring inside the apartment and then the door opened a crack.

When Adam realized who it was he opened the door wider and Taylor saw that he was standing there in his bathrobe, sleepily running a hand through his hair.

"Hi, honey." He yawned, cinching the belt of his robe more tightly around his waist.

"Oh, Adam, I'm sorry I woke you up," she apologized, closing the door behind her. "I didn't think you'd still be in bed."

He looked up at the clock on the wall with bleary eyes. "I should have been up an hour ago, anyway," he said, trying to convince himself of the fact.

"Adam! Adam! It came in the mail today!" she exclaimed, waving the letter in his face as she threw her arms around his neck. Seeing the confusion on his face, Taylor went on to explain. "I've been asked to be the principal cellist with the Chicago Symphony starting next season!"

"That's great, honey!" he exclaimed, his eyes opening wider. "Congratulations!" He returned her hug, dropping a light kiss on the tip of her nose. "Give me five minutes to shower and shave. Then you can tell me all about it," he proposed, rubbing a hand across the stubble of his beard.

"Better than that, I'll give you ten minutes *and* make you breakfast," she countered with a delighted laugh.

"Hmmm . . ." he murmured, nuzzling her neck, "maybe we should skip breakfast. You could always join me in the shower," he added in a drawl, his fingers tightening on her waist.

Taylor's eyes turned a hazy shade of blue-gray. "I've already had my shower, thanks," she declared a bit breathlessly. "Now behave yourself."

"What's the fun in that?" he asked seductively, his hands slipping down over her hips to press her into the cradle of his thighs.

Taylor felt her body responding to him as it always did. She leaned into him, her arms snaking beneath the robe to encircle his waist. "Don't you ever wear pajamas?" she began in a lecturing tone when she realized he was nude under the terrycloth robe.

"Pajamas are a confounded nuisance and a damned waste of time," Adam retorted. "Someday, my sweet, you'll realize that for yourself." Then he gently disengaged himself and turned and walked toward the bedroom. "You'll find some tea bags in the cupboard next to the refrigerator," he said over his shoulder.

"Since when do you keep tea bags on hand?" she called after him, puzzled by this innovation.

"Ever since I started going with a tea drinker," he called back, disappearing into the next room.

Well, she'd promised him breakfast and breakfast

he would get, Taylor thought. She folded the letter and stuck it in her handbag before going into the kitchen to rummage through Adam's refrigerator. She got out the bacon and eggs, deciding on traditional fare. She was briskly whipping the eggs and milk when she heard a familiar whistle from nearby.

"You always do wonders for a girl's ego, Rocky," she laughed, turning to glance at the small bird perched in his cage.

The eggs were scrambled and the bacon sizzling when Adam walked into the kitchen a prompt ten minutes later. Taylor turned to look over her shoulder and felt a jolt of electricity at the mere sight of the man. Good Lord, but she had it bad! Yes, she was in love with Adam. Yes, she wanted to be with him every minute their busy schedules allowed. But did she have to turn to jelly every time he walked into the room? She was becoming hopelessly dependent on him. She had recognized that fact for the past few weeks. It was getting to the point where she couldn't imagine a day without him in it.

"Smells good," Adam commented, leaning over her shoulder to take a whiff of the bacon frying in the pan on the stove.

"It'll be ready in just a minute," Taylor told him, watching as he took a mug from the cupboard and poured himself a cup of coffee.

The man was a damned public nuisance dressed like that, she grumbled to herself. The close-fitting jeans rode low on his hips, hugging his lean thighs and leaving little to the imagination. After all, she wasn't blind. She'd seen the way women looked at Adam. She was only very much afraid she looked at him in precisely the same way herself. Jealousy was one emotion she had always avoided like the plague. It was unreasonable and self-destructive. She knew Adam loved her, but maybe—just maybe—that wasn't enough anymore. Perhaps she needed commitment as well.

He was wearing the familiar red-plaid shirt with his jeans. A shirt she had once briefly worn herself that weekend in the mountains. At the thought of that weekend Taylor's heart skipped a beat. She wondered if Adam had deliberately chosen to wear that shirt today. She wouldn't put it past him. There was a storm brewing. She could feel it in the air as surely as she felt his eyes on her from across the kitchen.

"Aren't you going to eat anything?" he inquired as he noticed the table set for one.

Taylor shook her head. "Just a cup of tea. I had lunch a little while ago," she explained as she drained the strips of bacon on a paper towel. "You can sit down if you like. Everything is ready." She set the plate of bacon and eggs in front of him and sat down with her cup of tea.

"Thank you," Adam said politely. "One day you'll make a great wife for some lucky man." He looked up at her, his dark eyes openly issuing a challenge as surely as if he'd thrown down the gauntlet.

Taylor bit down hard on her lip. Didn't they say that discretion was the greater part of valor? Adam was goading her, deliberately trying to provoke her into starting an argument. He knew well enough that remarks like that made her blood boil. The question was *why?* Why was he trying to pick a fight with her?

She schooled her expression to show none of the exasperation she was feeling and calmly met his gaze.

"I don't think it can hurt for anyone to know how to cook," she replied, refusing to rise to the bait.

"So, tell me," Adam finally asked between bites, "when did this all start with the Chicago Symphony?"

"It didn't really start at any specific time," Taylor said carefully. "I've played with them a number of times as a guest artist over the years. They were always aware, I suppose, that I would like the chair as principal cellist if it ever became available. I read somewhere recently that the man currently in the position accepted an offer from the New York Philharmonic. I thought I might be considered, but I didn't know for sure until I got their letter in the mail today."

"I don't suppose you have to audition for this kind of thing," he said dryly.

"I'm a little beyond the auditioning stage in my career," she replied coolly. "They're well acquainted with my work."

"So, they make you the offer and you accept it. Is that it?" he asked in a voice devoid of any emotion.

Taylor acquiesced with a shrug. "In essence, yes, that's it." What did he expect her to say?

Adam sat back in his chair and took a drink of his coffee. "Will you be moving to Chicago?"

"Well, of course, I'll be moving to Chicago. It's a little far to commute," she flung back, losing her patience for just a moment. "Naturally, I'll finish the season here first," she went on, regaining her composure. "I won't be doing anything for the next six months or so."

"And then what?" Adam prompted in a low voice.

"And then I'll move to Chicago—probably sometime next summer." She watched as he got up to light a cigarette. Instead of returning to the table, he stood looking out the kitchen window, quietly smoking. "I-I thought you would be happy for me. I've worked so long and hard for just this kind of opportunity. Surely you don't expect me to turn it down?"

"No, I don't expect that of you," Adam said with grim humor. "And I am happy for you, Taylor," he said at last, turning around. "I guess I'm just wondering what will happen to us."

"To us?" she repeated, looking at him in bewilderment.

"Yes, *us!* You know, a man and a woman who are supposed to be in love with each other? As you said yourself, it's a little far to commute between here and Chicago."

"Well, actually, I thought we could talk about that," she began, moistening her bottom lip.

His eyebrows rose fractionally. "Talk about commuting?"

"No—talk about your moving to Chicago with me." There! She had finally said it!

Adam looked at her without saying a word. One minute stretched into two and then three. "And how do you propose I do that?" he asked at last. "My job happens to be here in Knoxville and unlike you I'm not expecting any imminent offers of a position with the Chicago police force."

"I know," Taylor mumbled, pausing to gather her wits. It must be handled delicately, very delicately indeed. "You see, I'll be selling my townhouse. I have a sizable amount invested in it and there's always a long waiting list of interested buyers." Adam stood there, waiting, apparently *not* seeing the point at all.

She tried again. "I should make a nice profit on the sale, and you told me you'd always wanted to study law. I-I thought you could use the money from the townhouse to put yourself through law school."

Something flickered in his eyes. His lips formed an obstinate line. "Don't you really mean *you* would be putting me through law school?"

"I suppose so, indirectly." She made the admission cautiously.

"It would hardly be indirect if I used your money," Adam replied with quick pride. "Thanks, anyway, but I'm not the kind of man who takes money from a woman," he grated, barely keeping his temper under control. "What the hell do you think I am? A damned gigolo?"

"No!" Taylor's frustration was summed up in that one word. What she had thought would be a skirmish was turning into a full-scale battle. "I don't think for a minute that you're a gigolo and to even suggest such a thing is an insult to us both." She got up from her chair and went to him, putting a hand on his arm. "Adam, I love you and you said you loved me, too. Don't you think you would try to do the same thing for me if the situation were reversed?"

He regarded her for a moment as if he suspected her of setting some sort of trap for him. "I might," he growled, but that was all he would admit to.

"Well, I think you would," she said softly. "Oh, darling, why can't you be reasonable about this?"

"I won't be kept by a woman!" Adam ground out as if that was the final word on the subject.

"You won't be kept by a woman!" Taylor exploded. It was like waving a red flag in front of her eyes. "Men keep women all the time, but I suppose in your book that's all right." Damn! She hadn't meant to say that. She had allowed Adam to sidetrack her from the real issue and now she'd gone and lost her temper. "I-I didn't mean for it to sound like that." She grimaced. "I thought we could be a partnership. It's done all the time, you know. I wouldn't be the first woman to put her husband through school."

"Husband?" Adam immediately latched on to the word. "You mean get married?" He looked intently into Taylor's eyes.

"That's how a man usually becomes a husband," she replied with a nonchalance she was far from feeling. Good God, she'd proposed to the man! "Haven't you ever thought about us getting married?" she asked in a low, fervent tone, not altogether sure she wanted to know the answer to that question. From the beginning the subject of marriage had been carefully circumvented by them both.

"Of course, I've thought about it." Suddenly, Adam's voice had become very quiet. "I've thought about it a hundred times in the past month." Taylor felt an incredible sense of relief flow through her body. "But what would I have to offer a woman like you?" he concluded, spreading his hands out in a gesture of resignation.

"Only the one thing I want most," she murmured softly. "Your love."

"No, I'm serious," he went on, waving that consideration aside. "What could I offer you? You already have your own home, your own car. You support yourself in a style far above anything I could ever afford on my salary. You don't need me, Taylor. You don't even need a husband."

"Is that what a husband is—someone who provides food and shelter?"

"That's the way it usually works," he observed, his tone dry and slightly brusque. "Let's face it, honey. The one thing I give you that you can't get on your own is sex. That's what you really need me for—what I can give you in bed."

Taylor closed her eyes and tried to think. This was worse than anything she had ever imagined. He couldn't believe that! "You can't actually believe that," she said in a hoarse whisper, opening her eyes, knowing he would see the pain, the hurt she was feeling. But all of a sudden she didn't care. He had hurt her. He had hurt her as no one else ever could.

"Don't look at me like that!" Adam rasped, his fingers digging into her shoulders.

"Don't look at you like what?" she asked in a lifeless voice, her shoulders slumping under the pressure of his hands.

"Don't look at me as if I'd just plunged a knife into your heart!" he told her savagely. Then he brought her to him, crushing her against his chest. "Oh, honey, don't you see it would never work for us? I'm beer and you're champagne. I'm the Rolling Stones and you're Bach and Debussy. No two people were ever more opposite than the two of us."

"I thought opposites were supposed to attract," she mumbled against his shirt.

"Oh, they attract all right," he said, half amused and half angry, "but that doesn't mean they should get married. God knows I've tried to see a future for us together, but I can't . . . I can't."

Taylor put her head back and looked up at him. "Adam, are you afraid to marry me?"

"Damn right I am!" he shot back at her. "The price is just too great."

"The price?" What price?

"A man isn't a man if he doesn't have his pride and self-respect. You may not believe it now, but sooner or later you would grow to hate a man like that." His voice was as cold as the wind in the dead of winter. "You don't need me, Taylor. You're young and beautiful and successful. You have your whole life ahead of you. You deserve the best and you should marry a man who can give it to you."

"How noble of you to care so much for what *you* think I need," she said, the tremor in her voice matching the tremor that ran down the length of her body. "But is it *your* pride or *my* welfare you're really thinking of? And what of love, Adam? What does all the rest matter if there isn't any love?"

"Sometimes love isn't enough," he stated cynically.

Taylor closed her eyes and shuddered. "I used to think that. Now I know that love is all there is," she murmured so quietly that he could barely hear her.

His eyes took on a hard sheen, his lips curling in a derisive grin. "Don't worry, honey. You'll love somebody else someday. Then you'll thank me."

"You'll have to excuse me, but gratitude is the last thing I'm feeling toward you right now," she said bitterly. "And you're wrong if you think I could ever love anyone but you. If you knew anything about the way I feel, then you could never say that." She dropped her hands and stepped away from him. "Maybe that's the real reason you won't marry me." She hadn't thought of it before, but it made sense somehow. "You don't really love me."

"I do love you." Adam's voice vibrated.

Taylor turned huge, sad eyes on him. "Then you don't love me enough. I would do anything for you. Can you say the same?"

Adam drew a breath and spoke slowly. "Anything, Taylor? Would you turn down the offer from Chicago?"

She had known he was going to say it and she hated him just a little for doing so. It was the one thing she didn't want him to ask of her. It was the one question she was afraid to ask herself. Did she love Adam enough to sacrifice the work of a lifetime? Did love demand that kind of sacrifice?

"That isn't fair," she whispered, desperation clearly in her voice.

Adam caught hold of her unceremoniously by the shoulder. "Lots of things aren't fair, honey. Life isn't fair."

"Don't talk to me as if I were some sheltered child!" Her voice was low, but weighted with disdain. "I might know more of life and its fairness or unfairness than you imagine, Adam." She speared him with a look. "Do all you policemen have this omnipotent 'I-know-better-than-thou' attitude or is it unique to Lieutenant Adam McCord?" That might be hitting below the belt, but she was hurting and she wanted him to hurt as well.

He winced. "I'm only trying to do what's best for you, babe, for both of us," Adam amended, his face gray with strain.

"Do me a favor," she said wearily. "*Don't* do me any more favors." The look on his face brought the tears to her eyes. She wasn't the only one in pain.

"Please don't cry, Taylor." His voice was unsteady as he reached for her.

"No!" she hissed, hardening her heart, putting a hand out to ward him off. "Don't touch me! I don't need you, remember? You told me so yourself." She turned and blindly made for the kitchen door.

He stopped her before she had gone two steps. "Where are you going?" he demanded.

Her face was white with distress. "I just want to be alone," she answered without turning around.

An indefinable expression crossed his face. "I'm not going to let you leave, Taylor—not like this."

She looked down at the strong hand grasping her arm. "And how will you keep me here, Adam? By force? That wouldn't do much for your precious self-respect and pride though, now would it?"

"Dammit, Taylor!" he swore under his breath, jerking his hand away as if he'd touched a hot coal.

"Or you could keep me here by making love to me." She stumbled over the words. "But I think I would hate you just a little bit if you did that, and I would loathe myself."

"Oh, honey, don't do this," he pleaded softly. "Stay here and we'll talk."

"No, Adam, I want to be by myself right now," she said in a small, firm voice. She picked up her handbag from a chair in the living room as she went by. She opened the door of his apartment and then turned to face him. "You know, you're wrong on both counts. We could have made it work and I do need you very much." Then Taylor turned and walked away, closing the door behind her.

She walked out of the apartment building and down

the sidewalk past her car and still she kept going. She could always get the car later. Right now she needed to walk. She needed to walk until she was too numb to think or even to feel.

She didn't notice the streetlights blink on as dusk fell on the city. She paid no heed when it clouded over and began to rain, lightly at first and then in a steady gray sheet that quickly soaked her to the skin. Some part of her mind operated on automatic, noting red lights and curbs and traffic. The rest of her gratefully accepted the mindless oblivion that came with physical exhaustion.

She walked until she had to concentrate on the simple task of putting one foot in front of the other to the exclusion of everything else. It was almost blissful to feel genuine physical pain. It was a welcome relief from the awful pain growing inside her.

Taylor never knew how far she walked or even where she went. She wandered for hours that night in the rain. She wasn't aware of anything until an insistent voice broke into her misery.

"Excuse me, miss. Are you all right?" Taylor heard the man's voice, but refused to turn her head to look at him.

"Do you think she's doped up or drunk, Joe?" asked the first man's companion.

"I don't know. I don't think so. She just looks kind of pathetic and lost. She sure doesn't look like she belongs in this part of town."

"Maybe we'd better take her down to the station," suggested the second man.

Perhaps it was the word "station" that finally penetrated the fog that clouded her brain. Whatever it was,

Taylor stopped and turned to look at the two patrolmen getting out of the black-and-white car.

"What's your name, miss?"

She didn't want to talk to any stranger, especially a policeman. The last time she had done that he had ended up breaking her heart.

"Where do you live?" the other officer asked.

Suddenly, she wanted to go home. The feeling was overwhelming. It was a feeling such as she had never known. She would be all right if she could only get home.

"24 Kenton Place," she recited. "I live at 24 Kenton Place."

The first officer looked at the second one. "I told you she wasn't from around here. What do you say we help her out by running her home? She'll never find a taxi around here at this time of night."

"We're going to take you home now," the other man told her as he settled her in the back seat of the police cruiser, tucking a blanket around her shivering form.

Taylor huddled in the back seat, watching the blur of lights as they drove through the night, suddenly realizing she was wet and tired and cold and very much alone.

In record time the police car was pulling up in front of her townhouse. It was ablaze with light from top to bottom. Funny, she didn't remember leaving the lights on. One of the patrolmen assisted her up the walk and was about to press the bell when the door flew open.

The officer standing beside her looked up. "Lieutenant McCord—I didn't expect to find you here!"

"Thank God, you've found her, Joe. Where was she? Is she all right?" It was Adam's voice, but somehow it sounded—different.

"We found her wandering around in the rain. She seems all right, but she's awfully wet and cold."

"I'll take care of her now," Adam reassured the man. "My fiancée has had a bad time of it today."

His fiancée? She wasn't anybody's fiancée. Why were they both talking about her as if she weren't even there? She was perfectly capable of speaking for herself.

"Thank you for bringing me home," Taylor said, turning to the uniformed man at her side.

"You're welcome, miss. Good night, Lieutenant." With that the patrolman was gone.

"He forgot his blanket," she murmured, taking it from around her shoulders and starting to go after him.

"Never mind, honey," Adam reassured her, coaxing her into the room. "I'll see that he gets it back."

She allowed him to lead her inside and then stood there a moment in the front hall—bedraggled, drenched to the skin, dripping water all over the beautiful hardwood floor, looking like a homeless waif if there ever was one.

"My God, Taylor, what have you done to yourself?" Adam rasped in a choked voice.

"I got wet," she said simply.

"Wet!" At that he sounded almost angry. "Do you have any idea what time it is?"

She raised her arm and looked at her wristwatch. It

didn't seem to be working. She tapped it with her finger. "My watch stopped."

"Your watch stopped?" Adam fiercely raked a hand through his hair. "You've been missing for hours and you tell me your watch stopped! It's nearly midnight, you little fool. You left my place over seven hours ago. Where in the hell have you been?"

9

Taylor suddenly felt confused, bewildered and more than a little lightheaded. "Where in the hell have I been?" She repeated his question slowly as if she intended to ponder the matter. "I've been walking." She looked at Adam to see if she had given the correct answer.

"You've been walking for seven hours?" he retorted with obvious skepticism.

"Seven hours?" She was suddenly confused all over again.

He took a menacing step toward her. "Taylor, have you been drinking?"

"Drinking? That's a good idea. Let's have a drink to warm us up." She turned and made for the cabinet in the living room where she kept an assortment of liquor.

"Oh, no, you don't!" An arm shot out to stop her. "A drink is the last thing you need right now. It's a hot shower for you, young woman."

She looked down at the hand firmly grasping her arm, then up to the stern face looming over her. "I don't need you to tell me what to do, Adam McCord. I don't need you at all. I don't need anyone. I can take care of myself," she declared with as much dignity as she could muster under the circumstances. "So you can just leave, mister! And take that burly chest of yours and your manly pride out the door with you." She swatted at him as if he were a persistent and particularly annoying insect. "I'm never going to take another shower as long as I live if I don't want to," she proclaimed irrationally.

"Right—" Just by the way he said the word she knew he didn't believe her.

"I mean it!" she raged at him, on the verge of losing her temper altogether.

"Sure you do, honey," he murmured in what sounded like a totally patronizing voice to her. "Now, c'mon, up the stairs we go."

Taylor shook off his hold. "I can do it by myself," she told him, determined to assert her independence. But when she faltered on the first step she found herself grateful for the supporting arm behind her. Not that she ever intended to let Adam know it.

"Time to get undressed and into a hot shower," he stated in a no-nonsense tone once they reached her bedroom. He stood her up by the end of the bed and started to unbutton the suit jacket plastered to her skin.

"I can do that," she growled at him.

"All right, then I'll turn the shower on while you get

your clothes off," Adam said with the impersonal tone of a physician dealing with an unreasonable patient.

He turned his back and stalked into the adjoining bathroom. A moment later she could hear the familiar sounds of the shower being turned on. It occurred to Taylor that she really should get out of her wet clothes before she caught pneumonia, but the bed behind her looked so inviting. Perhaps she could lie down for just a minute—just long enough to get some of her strength back. She stretched out, wet clothes and all, on top of the expensive designer spread. The damned thing could always be sent to the dry cleaners, she rationalized, not really caring what became of it.

"Leave me alone," she mumbled when insistent hands pulled her to her feet again. "I'm tired," she wailed helplessly. "I want to go to sleep."

"I know, honey, I know. And you can, just as soon as you get out of these wet things. God, your hands are frozen!" Adam hissed as he held them between his own.

"I don't care," she said in a childish, petulant voice. She opened her eyes a crack and watched as he undid the buttons down the front of her suit. "I hate it when you're nice to me," she said in the same thin, melancholy voice.

Adam took a deep, steadying breath. "Then you're just going to have to go on hating me because I intend to go on being nice to you for a long time."

"Why are you being nice to me, Adam?" she whispered hoarsely, her voice no more than a thin scratch of sound. "I-I thought you didn't like me anymore." There were sudden, hot tears at the corners of her eyes. She could feel them pricking her skin like sharp little needles.

"Of course I still like you," he reassured her in a roughly husky tone, pulling the rain-sodden skirt down over her hips. "Lift your foot."

She looked down at the skirt, now a wet heap around her ankles, and obediently did as he told her. "My stockings are ruined," she noted dispassionately.

"I'm afraid they're not all that's ruined," Adam observed, slipping the soggy leather shoes off her feet.

She made a disparaging sound through her clattering teeth. "I don't—"

"I know," he interrupted her. "You don't care if your shoes are ruined. You don't intend to ever wear shoes again unless you want to," he laughed darkly.

"I don't think that's amusing." She sniffed haughtily, trying to balance on one foot and finally having to resort to using his shoulder to steady herself. "I-I think you're almost enjoying this," she said accusingly as he slid the blouse off her arms and reached behind her to unclasp her bra.

"Believe me, there are dozens of things I'd enjoy more than undressing a soaking wet, not to mention uncooperative, woman who doesn't have the sense to come in out of the rain," Adam told her with grim humor, tugging at her wet panties.

"Adam!" She ineffectually tried to push his hand aside.

"This is hardly the time for false modesty, Taylor. I've seen it all before, remember?" His face was so close to hers she could see the darker brown rim around his brown eyes. "Now, into the shower with you and don't come out until I say so," he ordered with a pat to her bare backside.

For a moment she was tempted to stick her tongue out at him, but considering the vulnerable position she found herself in she decided that caution was the best policy. She settled for a meaningful glance over her shoulder that clearly relayed her feelings on the subject of his bossiness. "This is supposed to be a free country, not a dictatorship," she grumbled, stepping into the steamy shower.

Then she was lost in the hot, soothing spray that pelted her body, driving the chill from her bones. Taylor stood there for God knew how long, luxuriating in the simple fact that she was warm again. She poured a small pool of fragrant shampoo into her palm and gently worked it through her hair, letting the steady stream of water from the shower rinse it away. It was wonderful to feel clean again.

"You can come out now," she heard Adam call over the noise of the plumbing as he thrust a towel at her from around the edge of the plastic shower curtain.

"But I'm not ready to come out yet," she obstinately called back to him.

"You've been in there long enough, Taylor. You either come out on your own, or by God, I'm coming in to get you," he informed her in no uncertain terms.

"Yes sir, Lieutenant!" she mocked in a surly tone.

Taylor assumed he couldn't hear that last remark of hers. She was wrong. With one good yank, Adam pulled the shower curtain back and stood there glowering at her, hands planted on his hips.

He pointed to the mat on the bathroom floor. "Out!"

She thought of covering strategic parts of herself with her hands, but there didn't seem to be enough to go around.

"Could I please have my towel?" she ventured, making a grab for the one dangling from his hand.

She drew back when it became apparent he had no intention of parting with it. Instead, Adam took it upon himself to wrap the towel around her body, tucking in a corner above her breast to hold it in place.

"Now, sit." He pushed her down on the commode lid and began to rub her hair dry with a second towel.

"Ouch! You're rubbing too hard," she complained under his vigorous strokes.

He immediately relented. "Sorry—I haven't had much practice at this, I'm afraid. Besides, it's been a hell of a long night," he admitted in a weary growl.

"Were you really worried about me?" Taylor murmured, nibbling her bottom lip.

"Worried? Who me?" For a moment Adam tried to make light of it and failed. "I was out of my mind with worry," he spat out tightly. "I went kind of crazy when I found your car outside my apartment a couple of hours after you'd walked out."

"I-I didn't think it would be wise for me to drive just then," she managed in a shaky voice, telling him more than she realized. "I decided to take a walk."

"I wish I'd known that before I dialed your telephone number for two straight hours," he remarked, taking a brush to her hair.

"I'm sorry, Adam." It wasn't much. It certainly wasn't enough, but it was all Taylor could think of to say under the circumstances.

"I'm sorry, too, babe," he said softly. "I'm sorry for so damned many things I can't even begin to tell you all of them."

"Oh, Adam—" she choked, turning her face to rest it against his thigh.

She had caught him by surprise. His sharp intake of air told her that. But for a moment she continued pressing into his warmth and for a moment he allowed her to.

"C'mon, let's find a nightgown to put on you," Adam said quietly, drawing Taylor to her feet, his touch the slightest bit unsteady.

"Third drawer down on the right side," she told him when he raised his eyebrow in a questioning arch.

"You call these little bits of satin and lace nightgowns?" he asked as he rummaged through her drawer. "Don't you own even one decently warm flannel gown?"

At that, Taylor actually felt a smile tug at her mouth. "No one wears flannel nightgowns anymore. And who are you to talk? You don't even own a pair of pajamas," she snorted.

The intimacy of their conversation hit them simultaneously. Adam's eyes momentarily went black, his expression one of fleeting pain and desire. "Here, you'd better put this on," he muttered, picking a gown at random from the drawer. The time for false modesty long past, she dropped the towel without ceremony and stood nude before him. "For God's sake, Taylor, put it on!" Adam growled as if he'd come to the end of his rope.

Duly chastised, Taylor quickly slipped the nightgown on over her head. She hadn't meant to be provocative. At least that was what she tried to tell herself. "It's safe to turn around now," she told him with more than a hint of irony in her tone.

Adam suddenly became very active. He pulled the bedcovers back and gestured to her. "I want you to get in this bed and stay there while I go downstairs and make you a cup of hot tea." He proceeded to fluff her pillow and tuck the blankets snugly around her.

"One day you'll make a great father for some lucky child," she murmured, locking eyes with him.

"I'm working on it, lady," he mumbled, then turned to scoop up the pile of wet clothes from the floor. He was nearly out the bedroom door when he stopped and looked back at her. "I just remembered, you didn't have any dinner tonight, did you?" Taylor shook her head. "I'm not much of a cook as you know, but I think I could manage some buttered toast with that tea."

"Buttered toast sounds heavenly," she admitted, suddenly realizing she was hungry. "The toaster is in that large cupboard next to the stove. I keep the bread on the shelf above it and . . ."

"And don't tell me—you keep your butter in the refrigerator," he quipped with the first real show of amusement she had seen from him all evening. "I may not be much of a cook, honey, but give me some credit for being a good detective." Satisfied that he'd had the last word, Adam disappeared out the bedroom door.

She must have dozed off, for the next thing Taylor knew Adam was walking back in the room with a cup of tea in one hand and a plate of toast in the other. She quickly sat up in bed and made room for him to set it down on the nightstand beside her.

"This is the best tea and toast I've ever had," she exclaimed between bites. "Thank you, Adam. Did you have any problem finding things?"

"Where there's a will there's a way," he intoned, refusing to say any more on the subject. "Now, unless there's something else you need I think I'll head back to my apartment."

Suddenly, she was no longer hungry. "Aren't—

aren't you going to stay here tonight?" She tried to keep the quiver out of her voice.

"You need to sleep, Taylor," he said in an authoritative tone. "I think it would be best if I left. You only have to pick up the telephone if you need me."

She reached over and picked up the receiver of the telephone beside her bed. She didn't do it to be cute. She was dead serious.

"I lied to you earlier, Adam. I *do* need you. Not for just an hour or two, or a day, or a week, but for the rest of my life. And I need you tonight." There were some things worth sacrificing pride for. She wondered if he had discovered that yet.

His eyes stared straight through her. She could see him wavering between what he thought he should do and what he wanted to do. "All right, I'll stay—but on one condition."

"You're the boss," she said with no trace of irony in her voice.

"I will stay," Adam carefully enunciated each word, "if you promise to go to sleep."

Taylor executed a perfectly timed yawn. "I promise."

"Then finish your tea. It's late and we've both had a rough night," he pointed out needlessly. "I'm going downstairs to lock up and turn the lights off. I expect you to be asleep by the time I get back."

"Yes, Adam." And this time her yawn was for real. She handed the empty teacup over to him and snuggled down in the covers. "Thank you for taking care of me tonight," she murmured as her eyes fluttered closed.

He stood there looking down at her with an infinitely tender expression on his face. "God knows someone has to. It might as well be me," he softly whispered before walking away.

It was bitterly cold in bed and Taylor couldn't seem to find warmth anywhere. She was all alone and the immensity of that loneliness was unbearable. Where was Adam? He should be there, but she couldn't find him. She looked and looked. She looked everywhere, but he wasn't there.

"Adam!" Taylor shot up in bed with an awful start. It took her a moment to realize that the cry that had awakened her was her own.

"Taylor?" Her name was spoken softly. Then the light beside her bed was turned on and Adam was bending over her.

"I-I must have had a bad dream," she murmured, raising a trembling hand to her face. She looked up at him and saw that he, too, had been asleep. "I'm sorry I woke you up. That makes twice in one day, doesn't it?" she said with grim humor.

"It doesn't matter. The chair wasn't that comfortable anyway," he remarked dryly, rubbing a spot low on his back.

"Chair?" Taylor looked around her bedroom and spotted his shoes beside the lounge chair in the corner. "Oh, Adam, you've been sitting up all night," she whispered guiltily.

He shrugged unconcernedly. "It wouldn't be the first time and it won't be the last." Then he grimaced and rubbed his back again. "Of course, I'm not getting any younger. Scoot over, will you?"

She quickly made room for him beside her. He stretched out on the bed face down and exhaled a long sigh. "Your clothes look like you've slept in them," Taylor observed with a gentle smile. Then she reached out and began to massage his lower back. She knew when she hit the right spot by Adam's groan of appreciation.

"Keep this up and I promise to marry you first thing in the morning," he mumbled into the covers. Taylor's movements stopped abruptly. Adam turned his head and caught the pained expression on her face before she turned away. "I'm sorry, honey. That was a hell of a stupid thing to say," he growled, reaching for her. He held her for a moment and then caught her chin in his hand and gently coerced her to look at him. "I was going to save this until morning, but I think we'd better talk now."

"I don't know what we could possibly have to talk about," she said defensively. "I thought we'd done all our talking yesterday."

"I'll admit I deserve that one," Adam muttered, pushing himself up to sit beside her. "Taylor, I love you," he said without preamble. "I love you and I need you," he went on in his softest tone. "And I found out last night that you need me, too." He permitted himself a small sigh. "I guess there are different ways of needing someone and they aren't always the obvious ones. The important thing between any man and woman is that they satisfy each other's needs, whatever they may be."

Taylor looked at him, still skeptical. "Do you really mean that?" Was it possible, after all, for a leopard to change his spots?

Adam nodded. "I did a lot of thinking after you left my apartment yesterday. I said some pretty stupid things to you and I know I hurt you badly, but I'll make it up to you. I promise."

"There's no need for that," she assured him. "I said

some pretty stupid things myself. You may have noticed that subtlety isn't always my strong point."

"Well, now that you mention it, you do have a little bit of a tendency to lecture, my sweet. A man likes to be *asked,* not *told.*"

"I guess it's the teacher in me," she sighed in acknowledgment. It was his turn next. "And you, my darling man, have a tendency to order me around as if I were one of your subordinates."

"I guess it's the lieutenant in me," he echoed. "It did finally occur to me that I was penalizing you for being successful. I've always admired your talent and the fact that you've worked hard to get where you are. Then when I had to accept the results of that hard work I threw it in your face." Adam looked at her with a loving expression he made no attempt to hide. "You're a very special woman, Taylor Jameson, with a very special gift. You should use that gift to its greatest extent. I can honestly say that I want you to go to Chicago and be the best principal cellist they've ever had."

"And?" Taylor waited for him to go on, scarcely daring to breathe.

"And I've decided that loaning me the money to go to law school may be the best investment you've ever made. The return on your investment will last a lifetime and I intend to repay you with interest."

"Hmmm . . . I like the part about the *interest,*" she murmured, moving closer.

"We'll be a partnership," Adam was telling her as he began to stroke her arm. "You know, you scratch my back now, I'll scratch yours later. We may decide to have children in a few years, and a hardworking lawyer could do well by his family."

"I would say he could do very well," she told him encouragingly. "I'd like one of each," Taylor added wistfully.

"One of each?" Adam looked down at her, puzzled.

"A boy and a girl."

"The perfect compromise," he smiled meaningfully. "And that's what love is, isn't it? The perfect compromise."

Taylor's eyes shone with the full force of her love. "I've always enjoyed *compromising* you," she drawled, turning to kiss his throat.

"In the middle of the night, my love?" he teased, nuzzling the soft curls at her nape.

"It's not the middle of the night anymore," she pointed out as she went into his arms. "I think I see the dawn breaking on the horizon now."

"In that case, what better way to start the day?" Adam chuckled at his own rhyme, his hands searching beneath the covers for her gentle, sloping curves.

Her own hands went to the buttons of his shirt as Taylor began to undress him with a light and loving touch. When she reached the buckle at his waist Adam became impatient, rolling away from her long enough to remove the rest of his clothing. He stood there for a moment in his natural glory, gazing down at her with eyes that spoke of love and passion.

"Please come to bed, Adam," she breathed, holding her arms out to him in invitation.

It was an invitation he accepted eagerly, willingly, lovingly, going into her arms as he took her into his. His kiss was a tender vow that quickly became a burning desire between them, a desire to give as well as to receive, to excite as well as satisfy. There was a new element in their lovemaking this time, a kind of sweet desperation, as if they suddenly realized how close they had come to losing each other and the wondrous, unending madness that happened between them with a kiss and a touch.

Adam threw the covers aside, and when she shivered at the first contact of cool, morning air on her skin, he covered her with his own body. "I'll keep you warm, my sweet Taylor, so very warm," he vowed.

First there was the heat of his kiss on her mouth and then on the curve of her neck and finally on the soft rise of her breast above the satin gown. He nudged the bodice gently aside, his touch burning her bare flesh, stoking the flames of her desire. His tongue moistened the tip until it ached for the sweet release he promised. But the flames only burned higher as his lips surrounded her, his teeth teasing the taut center into an ever-hardening proof of her arousal.

His hands slowly slid the satin gown down her body, his caress following in its wake until a trail of fire extended from her breast to the soft flesh between her thighs. He made her his with the touch of his hands and the hunger of his mouth. She was wild with the need he created in her, and she expressed that need with her own hands, her own mouth, her own tongue.

"My God, Taylor!" Adam cried out as her lips sought the intimate warmth of him. Then he reached down and pulled her along the length of his body until his breath was harsh against her mouth. "I need you! I need you now!" he rasped, molding his mouth to hers.

"And I need you," Taylor declared with all her heart. "I need you now and always!"

"I will love you always," he promised as he eased his weight down on her, seeking to fulfill that promise by making them one, by taking her with him into a world of their own where now and always and forever existed in each moment.

His body surged against hers and she responded instantly. He mastered her feminine softness, only to find himself enslaved. He sought to give her pleasure and found his own in the giving. And in the beginning of the end, they clung to one another and fearlessly faced the world together, finding as man and woman the ageless answer to the ageless question.

They still clung to each other as the first light of a new dawn broke across the sky, savoring this moment between night and day, basking in the warmth of their love, a love that would give them the strength to meet each new day and whatever came after.

"I've always said you were a very special woman," Adam murmured, holding her close to his heart.

"Only because you're a very special man," Taylor assured him lovingly.

"Even if I'm a little bossy now and then?" he chuckled. It was a cozy, intimate sound.

"Oh, I think I can handle a little bossiness, Lieutenant. As long as it doesn't get out of hand."

"And if it does?" he gently challenged.

"Well, in that case," she drawled, running a finger along his thigh, "I'd be forced to take the law into my own hands. . . ."

And she did to his everlasting delight.

YOU'LL BE SWEPT AWAY WITH SILHOUETTE DESIRE

$1.75 each

1 ☐ CORPORATE AFFAIR
James

2 ☐ LOVE'S SILVER WEB
Monet

3 ☐ WISE FOLLY
Clay

4 ☐ KISS AND TELL
Carey

5 ☐ WHEN LAST WE
LOVED
Baker

6 ☐ A FRENCHMAN'S KISS
Mallory

7 ☐ NOT EVEN FOR LOVE
St. Claire

8 ☐ MAKE NO PROMISES
Dee

9 ☐ MOMENT IN TIME
Simms

10 ☐ WHENEVER I LOVE
YOU Smith

$1.95 each

11 ☐ VELVET TOUCH
James

12 ☐ THE COWBOY AND
THE LADY Palmer

13 ☐ COME BACK, MY
LOVE Wallace

14 ☐ BLANKET OF STARS
Valley

15 ☐ SWEET BONDAGE
Vernon

16 ☐ DREAM COME TRUE
Major

17 ☐ OF PASSION BORN
Simms

18 ☐ SECOND HARVEST
Ross

19 ☐ LOVER IN PURSUIT
James

20 ☐ KING OF DIAMONDS
Allison

21 ☐ LOVE IN THE CHINA
SEA Baker

22 ☐ BITTERSWEET IN
BERN Durant

23 ☐ CONSTANT
STRANGER Sunshine

24 ☐ SHARED MOMENTS
Baxter

25 ☐ RENAISSANCE MAN
James

26 ☐ SEPTEMBER
MORNING Palmer

27 ☐ ON WINGS OF NIGHT
Conrad

28 ☐ PASSIONATE
JOURNEY Lovan

29 ☐ ENCHANTED DESERT
Michelle

30 ☐ PAST FORGETTING
Lind

31 ☐ RECKLESS PASSION
James

32 ☐ YESTERDAY'S
DREAMS Clay

33 ☐ PROMISE ME
TOMORROW Powers

34 ☐ SNOW SPIRIT
Milan

35 ☐ MEANT TO BE
Major

36 ☐ FIRES OF MEMORY
Summers

37 ☐ PRICE OF SURRENDER
James

38 ☐ SWEET SERENITY
Douglass

39 ☐ SHADOW OF
BETRAYAL Monet

40 ☐ GENTLE CONQUEST
Mallory

41 ☐ SEDUCTION BY
DESIGN St. Claire

42 ☐ ASK ME NO SECRETS
Stewart

43 ☐ A WILD, SWEET
MAGIC Simms

44 ☐ HEART OVER MIND
West

45 ☐ EXPERIMENT IN LOVE
Clay

46 ☐ HER GOLDEN EYES
Chance

47 ☐ SILVER PROMISES
Michelle

48 ☐ DREAM OF THE WEST
Powers

49 ☐ AFFAIR OF HONOR
James

Silhouette Desire

- 50 ☐ FRIENDS AND LOVERS Palmer
- 51 ☐ SHADOW OF THE MOUNTAIN Lind
- 52 ☐ EMBERS OF THE SUN Morgan
- 53 ☐ WINTER LADY Joyce
- 54 ☐ IF EVER YOU NEED ME Fulford
- 55 ☐ TO TAME THE HUNTER James
- 56 ☐ FLIP SIDE OF YESTERDAY Douglass
- 57 ☐ NO PLACE FOR A WOMAN Michelle
- 58 ☐ ONE NIGHT'S DECEPTION Mallory
- 59 ☐ TIME STANDS STILL Powers
- 60 ☐ BETWEEN THE LINES Dennis
- 61 ☐ ALL THE NIGHT LONG Simms
- 62 ☐ PASSIONATE SILENCE Monet
- 63 ☐ SHARE YOUR TOMORROWS Dee

- 64 ☐ SONATINA Milan
- 65 ☐ RECKLESS VENTURE Allison
- 66 ☐ THE FIERCE GENTLENESS Langtry
- 67 ☐ GAMEMASTER James
- 68 ☐ SHADOW OF YESTERDAY Browning
- 69 ☐ PASSION'S PORTRAIT Carey
- 70 ☐ DINNER FOR TWO Victor
- 71 ☐ MAN OF THE HOUSE Joyce
- 72 ☐ NOBODY'S BABY Hart
- 73 ☐ A KISS REMEMBERED St. Claire
- 74 ☐ BEYOND FANTASY Douglass
- 75 ☐ CHASE THE CLOUDS McKenna
- 76 ☐ STORMY SERENADE Michelle
- 77 ☐ SUMMER THUNDER Lowell
- 78 ☐ BLUEPRINT FOR RAPTURE Barber

- 79 ☐ SO SWEET A MADNESS Simms
- 80 ☐ FIRE AND ICE Palmer
- 81 ☐ OPENING BID Kennedy
- 82 ☐ SUMMER SONG Clay
- 83 ☐ HOME AT LAST Chance
- 84 ☐ IN A MOMENT'S TIME Powers
- 85 ☐ THE SILVER SNARE James
- 86 ☐ NATIVE SEASON Malek
- 87 ☐ RECIPE FOR LOVE Michelle
- 88 ☐ WINGED VICTORY Trevor
- 89 ☐ TIME FOR TOMORROW Ross
- 90 ☐ WILD FLIGHT Roszel

SILHOUETTE DESIRE, Department SD/6
1230 Avenue of the Americas
New York, NY 10020

Please send me the books I have checked above. I am enclosing $_____
(please add 50¢ to the cover postage and handling. NYS and NYC residents please add appropriate sales tax.) Send check or money order—no cash or C.O.D.'s please. Allow six weeks for delivery.

NAME _____

ADDRESS _____

CITY _____ STATE/ZIP _____

Get 6 new
Silhouette Special Editions
every month
for a 15–day FREE trial!

Free Home Delivery, Free Previews, Free Bonus Books.
Silhouette Special Editions are a new kind of romance
novel. These are big, powerful stories that will capture
your imagination. They're longer, with fully developed
characters and intricate plots that will hold you spellbound from the first page to the very last.

Each month we will send you six exciting *new*
Silhouette Special Editions, just as soon as they are published. If you enjoy them as much as we think you will,
pay the invoice enclosed with your shipment. **They're
delivered right to your door with never a charge for
postage or handling, and there's no obligation to buy
anything at any time.** To start receiving Silhouette Special
Editions regularly, mail the coupon below today.

Silhouette Special Edition

Silhouette Special Editions,® **Dept. SESD 7S**
120 Brighton Road, Clifton, NJ 07012

Please send me 6 Silhouette Special Editions, absolutely free,
to look over for 15 days. If not delighted, I will return only 5
and owe nothing.

NAME_____

ADDRESS_____

CITY_____

STATE_____ ZIP_____

SIGNATURE_____
(If under 18, parent or guardian must sign.)
This offer expires April 30, 1984

Silhouette Special Editions ® is a registered trademark of Simon & Schuster